T0114542

MARS
HORIZON

MARS HORIZON

Thomas DePhillipo

authorHOUSE®

AuthorHouse™
1663 Liberty Drive
Bloomington, IN 47403
www.authorhouse.com
Phone: 1 (800) 839-8640

Published by AuthorHouse   09/25/2015

ISBN: 978-1-5049-5014-5 (sc)
ISBN: 978-1-5049-5345-0 (e)

Print information available on the last page.

TABLE OF CONTENTS

LIST OF ILLUSTRATIONS

Special thanks to my wife Jennifer, my kids Alexis and Tom for their encouragement and many suggestions about this story.

Acknowledgements

Illustration Acknowledgments and credits:
Martian Greenhouse - NASA
Cover – NASA/JPL
Sky Crane – NASA/JPL
First Stage Cargo Section – NASA
Hybrid Vehicle - NASA
Dream Machine in Flight - NASA
Martian Landscape - NASA

FORWARD

This book was written with the help of imaginary alter egos drawn from some of my friends. I only used very basic personality characteristics and interests, as I knew them, like a scaffold to build on all of the fictional traits and experiences of the characters in the book. Any resemblance beyond a superficial similarity, whether intentional or not, is purely coincidental and has no basis in real life.

PROLOGUE

MARS…...the mysterious red planet…… with canals cratered into its landscape has been the subject of mankind's speculation for ages. Over the centuries Martian lore has grown and thrived like other mysteries born in antiquity, waiting for the quintessential moment of discovery, the right time and circumstances coming together to reveal the true nature of the red planet.

Dark Energy accounts for 72% of all the energy in our world. This mysterious and little understood force is all around us and is responsible for causing the expansion of the universe. Until recently it was assumed that immediately after the big bang the expansion of the universe began slowing, ultimately destined to collapse in the big crunch, but space based Doppler measurements have now confirmed the universe is in fact expanding and at an accelerating rate. Like an invisible antigravity force Dark Energy is pushing all of the objects in the cosmos further apart, constantly enlarging the emptiness of space.

Early in the 21st century a small R&D firm accidentally stumbled upon a life changing discovery, having the potential to alter the way mankind lives and works on earth and in particular travels around our solar system and beyond. While testing a unique shaped charge design, an extremely high energy plasma jet caused a change in the nuclear structure of the target material, allowing it to react with Dark Energy. The discovery became the key to understanding the nature of dark energy and the beginning of a search to identify how best to use this new power source. It was an elegant design that defied credibility other than to say that it would work anywhere in the universe.

For over a decade the US Government had been looking for ways and means to travel to Mars. Mars is 60 million miles from Earth at its closest point and would take approximately one year for a spaceship using current technology, to make a one-way trip. This daunting task would require a huge investment and a tremendous risk to any astronauts attempting the flight. The same trip could be made in one week using this new energy source, with minimal risks due to the lack of tons of explosive fuels and the ability to quickly make a rescue mission in the event of an emergency. In addition, the investment required would be an order of magnitude less than using standard rocket technology while providing the means to transport large quantities of equipment, materials and provisions that would be needed for extended stays on Mars.

Seizing upon this new propulsion system commercial preparations immediately began to not only land a man on Mars but to establish a permanent Martian Base. To facilitate living conditions on the red planet it was planned to land on a known ice pack and drill into it extracting an endless supply of water. Breaking down the water into its oxygen and hydrogen components would provide the means for extended stays in a habitable environment and the energy source for powering the heavy equipment brought on the trip.

Fueled by competing interests from the Government and established Aerospace companies, behind the scenes intrigue constantly threatened the mission, the people and the personal fortunes involved. Aside from the technical challenges that posed a danger, nothing compared to the invisible threat posed by the Government. Driven by money and greed history is scared by the conflicts waged by nations over energy commodities such as Big Oil and Nuclear Power. Only this time they would pale by comparison; you'd have to go back to the invention of the wheel for the kind of impact this discovery would hold for civilization.

Despite the dangers the mission progressed and subsequent trips would further build-up and expand these early Martian settlements. This marks the beginning of colonizing an alien planet and the genetic adaptations of the first Martian explorers creating a truly Martian population. The details and progression of this new propulsion system, traveling thru space and the Martian base are contained in the following chapters.

Chapter 1

THE DISCOVERY

ArmorTec labs May 24 2016; it was the final day of testing the most recent variation of Hyper-Jet, ArmorTec's proprietary new shaped charge design. If successful the promise of lucrative military supply contracts would certainly be assured. We had been working on this for several years and had stretched the company's and my own personal financial resources to the limit; everything was now riding on Hyper Jet. At 8 am sharp I arrived at our test facility. Jim Dougherty our field supervisor was directing the setup of the latest and greatest version of hyper jet to defeat a particularly hard depleted uranium armor panel. We had hopes of not only penetrating the 8 inch thick target but also expected to vaporize the material at the point of impact.

"Hey Jim," I yelled, "are we ready yet?"

"Almost Mr. D, just synchronizing the radar guns so we get a clean picture." Another half hour passed before we were ready and my stomach was beginning to growl. I hadn't eaten anything and the anticipation was getting to me.

"OK" Jim hollered, "everybody in the bunker we're good to go." The bunker was a rehabbed transportation container behind a 9 foot high earthen berm. A wire-way from the test stand was threaded into the base of the bunker and fed inside to a variety of electronic equipment for detonating and recording the path of the plasma jet from initiation to impact. The top of the container was covered with over a foot of dirt and required wood supports to prevent the roof from sagging. Inside smelled like a rusty can, I always stood near the rear door wondering how the hell the roof hadn't collapsed yet. Once the field techs were all inside a final calibration check was made and an outside blast claxon sounded 3 times. Jim looked over at me and nodded, I nodded back. Jim hollered

"Fire in the hole" and detonated the charge. I instantly felt the blast pressure and the bunker shook for an instant dropping a mist of dirt from the ceiling. We immediately came out of the bunker to examine the test panel. Jim looked at it first, I saw his shoulders droop and a frown came over his face. "Not so good Mr. D" he whispered, He knew how much the test meant. I felt the knot in my stomach tighten and started to sweat,

"Just another test" I stuttered "we'll get it next time," wondering if there would be a next time. "Jim, wrap this up ASAP and get me the x-rays, I've got to figure out where we go from here."

"Sure thing Mr. D, You'll have my report this afternoon."

Jim Dougherty was a special forces Vet having served 3 tours of duty in Afghanistan and Iraq and began working for ArmorTec right out of the service. An ordnance specialist and an excellent marksman, Jim had all the qualifications I wanted to handle our testing operations. He also was a professional, knew how to take orders and give them. The field techs respected him and he imposed his own brand of discipline at the test site. "No bullshit, just do the job and follow procedures" he would say. Under his supervision we had a perfect safety record and Jim meant to keep it that way. He knew first-hand what an explosive device could do to the human body having earned 2 Purple Hearts and a slew of other combat medals.

Back at the office my secretary Marie, walked in with a cup of coffee in one hand and the day's mail in the other.

"Thanks Marie, anything besides bills?"

"No Tom, nothing that can't wait, how did the test go?" With a disgusted look I muttered

"OK not exactly what I expected."

"Too bad" she sighed "you'll get it next time." That's what I said to Jim, I thought. Marie looked worried; she knew better than me our financial situation and probably also wondered would there be a next time.

Marie was an attractive 40 something and a single mom, she needed the job and I liked having her around. It always got my attention the way she turned and swayed out of my office.

"Look" I said "things always seem worse than they are. We still have a healthy backlog of work, but Hyper Jets been a drain; it's all in-house funded and maybe we should put it on the back burner."

"Whatever you say Tom you'll get it, you always have." I smiled and intently watched as she left my office. Five minutes later the phone rang, it was Jim.

"Mr. D. I think you should come back to the firing range right away,"

"Anything wrong?" I asked,

"Nothing wrong, but we have a very unusual condition with the test panel we shot today."

"What is it, is it good or bad?"

"I'm not sure you'll have to see for yourself."

"I'm on my way" I said and hung up.

Driving back to the range I thought how strange Jim sounded and out of character not offering any explanation. Jim had always referred to me as Mr. D and maintained a formal relationship, I guessed, a habit from his military background. In any event we started that way and it stuck. A half hour later I pulled into the range and saw Jim waiting for me at the parking lot.

"Hey what's all the mystery about?"

"I can't explain it Mr. D never saw anything like it, the damn test panel weighs a ton."

"So" I asked, and to my astonishment Jim replied

"it started out at a half ton."

"Must be a mistake Jim are you sure?"

"No way, it's a standard size panel and they all weigh pretty much the same. I knew something was wrong when we pulled it off the test stand with the small lift and it practically tilted it over." There was a commotion at the test stand, the techs were standing around the test panel arguing and laughing. "What the hell's going on" Jim interrupted,

"you're not going to believe this Jim" the lead tech said, "we managed to flip the panel to examine the exit side and now it weighs less than 500 pounds."

"That's impossible," Jim insisted, "show me." The range property had a commercial scale mounted on a concrete platform about 1 foot above the ground, the exit side of the panel was already in place and the scale read 486 pounds. "OK" Jim ordered, "now flip it on the opposite side." I couldn't help noticing the difficulty the techs had, holding the panel over the scale while the lift was flipping it over. It seemed to be deflecting sideways and it took 3 men to hold it in place. The panel now lay flat with the impact side up and again to my astonishment the scale read 1,780 pounds, almost four times as much as the flip side. I looked at Jim and said

"this is crazy but maybe it's a good crazy, I need to get some metallurgical experts in here. Let's keep this quiet until we figure it out otherwise we'll all wind up in the loony bin."

"Sure thing Mr. D, what do you want to do with the panel?"

"Just cover it for now and mark it classified."

Phil Vizi was an old school chum who had earned his PHD in Physics and specialized in metallurgy. He worked at NASA during the transition years to commercial space flight now dominated by Internet Moguls looking for the next big thing. Phil was top notch in his field and regularly consulted with the new core of near earth space flight companies. It was Saturday and I called Phil at home to avoid any work distractions; it usually took a day or two before he responded to voice mail at his office.

"Hello Phillip how the hell are you?"

"Hey Tom long time no talk what's going on?"

"I've got an interesting problem I'd like you to look at."

"Hope it doesn't involve a dog," Phil laughed, "the last time you called on a weekend I had to bail your ass out of jail for punching your neighbor."

"Yea, that was embarrassing, but nobody kicks my dog, the bastard deserved it…. listen Phil, this is something special, I mean real special, I need your help."

"Sure Tom, what do you need?"

"Meet me at ArmorTec's range on Monday morning," I replied, "you have to see this for yourself, you wouldn't believe me if I told you."

"OK, OK, I'll be there, see you on Monday."

Phil knew I could be over the top at times but I could always count on him for help with any of my spontaneous ventures, however crazy they appeared. As college freshmen, I came to class one day with boxes of cologne bottles labeled "La Gondola the Italian Canoe." Canoe was a trade name for a popular cologne at the time and my brother and I had a local chemist whip up a batch that closely duplicated the scent.

"Here" I said, "just splash it on everyone that passes by and sell it for a buck a bottle" –

"One dollar?" Phil asked, "what the hell's in it for me?"
"Stock" I said confidently "as an original sales associate you're entitled to a share of the profits, we'll make a fortune." Phil skeptically nodded and started spraying anyone who came within 5 feet of him. Surprisingly they liked it and we quickly sold out. The next day Phil was confronted by most of the guys that bought wanting their money back.

"Now what" Phil yelled at me,

"just tell them if they used it they bought it, no returns" I yelled back. Apparently the witch's brew that our chemist whipped up had a very high alcohol content and other cheap chemicals in order to save costs, it went on fine and smelled like Canoe for about 10 minutes and then quickly evaporated…. End of the cologne business. Phil was embarrassed, his first commercial failure he thought at the time and now 25 years later, despite a stellar career at NASA, he was still looking for that first commercial success.

Arriving at ArmorTec's range Phil quickly found me drinking coffee outside the blast bunker.

"Want some" I asked raising my cup.

"No thanks, already had my quota for the day, now what's all the secrecy about." I briefly described the weight differential exhibited by the target panel before and after testing and pressed Phil for a possible answer. "Now hold on, I can't even speculate what possibly caused this without a detailed examination. First of all, assuming this is not bullshit or some screw-up your team made, I'll need some sample material right from the impact area, we'll break it down at our lab, run some mass spectroscopy tests and take a look at its molecular structure under an electron beam microscope. Get it back to me today and I'll start on it tomorrow, how's that sound?" looking relieved, I replied

"Feel better already." Walking back to his car, Phil cautioned,

"Tom I don't have to tell you how strange this is or sounds, if I were a gambling man I'd bet on a mistake, don't want you to be too disappointed."

"Don't worry," I replied, "my gut tells me this is for real."

A FedEx package arrived at NASA's satellite lab facility where Phil worked first thing Tuesday morning. The package from ArmorTec contained several metal granular samples each individually wrapped and annotated with an average grain size. Phil immediately carried the samples to the spectroscopy lab and walked in.

"Good morning John got some samples I'd like you to prep and analyze."

"OK Phil just leave them, I should have some time tomorrow."

"Unh Unh" Phil insisted, "this is top priority, need it ASAP." With that several lab techs began the process of micronizing, reducing the material to its smallest grain size possible. While collecting the micronized samples, to everyone's surprise a blue haze was observed hovering over the sample. It turned out to be an electron cloud indicating an unstable condition. "This is interesting" Phil said in a suspicious tone of voice, "it takes a lot of energy to do this, where the hell did it come from?"

"Got me" replied John, "let's see what spectroscopy comes up with." A half hour passed before the print out from the mass spectrometer cranked out, indicating a range of steel alloy elements but no depleted uranium. The results were inconsistent with the known composition of the material and after several reruns the results were the same.

"I want to get a closer look at this" Phil quipped, walking over to the EB microscope. Focusing in on a sample at 10 millionth power the molecular structure appeared normal except for one portion of the alloy. It looked like depleted uranium but had a small variation and it seemed to be changing right before his eyes. "I'll be dammed" he muttered, "I do believe we have a mutation,"

"a mutant steel alloy?" John questioned. "Can't be, this is inanimate stuff."

"Yea well tell that to the sample, I've got to get back to ArmorTec and find out more about their Hyper Jet program." Walking into our lobby Phil spotted my secretary getting ready to leave, "Hi Marie is the boss in?"

"Oh hi Mr. Vizi, he's always in, I know he'll be glad to see you." Slouching behind my desk over a stack of papers, the organized chaos of my daily routine was interrupted; "wake up boy" Phil hollered, "looks like you have something."

"Son of a bitch, I knew it" I anxiously replied jumping up, "what did you find out?"

"In a nutshell we have an extraneous energy source and a mutant alloy for starters."

"What I need to understand now is Hyper Jet, what is it and what does it produce?" Phil asked.

"Right" I said, "it's a shaped charge which is a focused explosive device that forms a high speed jet," Phil interrupted,

"Tom I know what a shape charge is and how it works tell me why Hyper Jet is different."

"Sorry, well then you're familiar with the copper conical liner that forms the primary plasma jet for penetrating armor. Hyper Jet employs the collision of multiple primary jets to form a secondary jet with extremely higher speeds causing a third order impact."

"OK you're losing me now, what is a third order impact?" I went on,

"If you place a bulk explosive charge on a chunk of steel and detonate it the plate will bend, maybe break, that's a first order impact. A second order impact, typical of a conventional shaped charge has a plasma jet that travels at 3000 meters a second and penetrates armor plate like a straw going thru warm butter. A third order impact, ala Hyper Jet, develops a plasma jet traveling at 20,000 meters a second that vaporizes armor plate generating radiation effects; we think its emitting gamma rays."

"Impressive" Phil said, "What kind of temperatures are you getting?"

"Comparable to the inside of the sun"……..

"Hmm, I'm beginning to understand Tom, extreme conditions like that may be enough to break down a material at the atomic level and rearrange its molecular structure into something else. The next step is to find out what that something else is."

Phil was a good scientist, maybe even a great one; he picked up on this right away. You could see his brain working, logically matching observations with test data, quickly ferreting thru plausible explanations and ways to validate conclusions. I needed someone like that who could fix my screw ups but I knew ArmorTec could not afford to get bogged down into an endless scientific investigation. We had a proof of concept and I owned it. Making it work and applying it was where I wanted to go even if we didn't know how it worked.

I spent the next week holed up in my office often till late at night trying to come up with a plan and the resources to use our repelling armor plate. Instinctively I knew, if we could synthesize and apply the sample material to any surface, with the power developed appearing to be directional, I would have a machine, the most efficient machine in the world. It wouldn't require any fuel, have no moving parts and be able to operate in any environment. Not bad, I thought, all I needed was lots of money. The government had the resources although likely agencies such as NASA and DOD were facing major funding cut backs, besides any technology investments made by the government at this level and I would lose control for any follow on work. The real applications and money would be reserved for the big boys, Lockheed Martin, Boeing, Hughes and the like. Not a good idea, at least not with this. Venture Capitalists could do it but the technology was not mature enough to leave me with any control as a first stage funding candidate. I needed an angel, a financial angel that had deep pockets; a Techy with a big enough ego to gamble on a wild idea.

After a weekend at my shore house I had a chance to recharge my batteries. The hectic pace that I had been on was getting to me and I needed to step back and set some priorities. I was determined to find a way to get Phil Vizi more involved, he was too good of an asset to remain on the sidelines. Next would be to rearrange company finances for an all-out push to recreate the mutant molecule in a form that could be commercially applied. If successful I was confident we could raise the funding to build my magic machine and if not I was also sure it would be the end of ArmorTec. All or nothing again, I had been there several times in my career. It always made you feel more alive more passionate, to believe in something and I felt lucky to be there, only this time I was sure the brass ring would not pass my way again.

I arrived at my office late Monday morning. Marie was on the phone and whispered as I passed by her desk,

"Be with you in a minute,"

"No hurry" I replied and closed my door. I called Phil at his office and left a voicemail thinking I may hear back by midweek. I had no sooner hung up and my direct line rang, it was Phil.

"Morning Tom glad you called we've got lots to talk about."

"Me first Phil, I want to put a team together to develop the repelling panel concept and I want you to lead the team; what do you think?" Phil was silent for a long moment,

"Caught me by surprise Tom, you know I'm interested but I can't see me as an employee, wouldn't work out."

"What did you have in mind?" I asked,

"Tom like you I've got more miles behind me than in front. I really believe you've got something here that's important and I want to be a part of it but as a partner with a piece of the action."

"Well" I began," Phil interrupted,

"I'm prepared to invest, and carry my own weight."

"Easy Phil, I'd be glad to take you on as a partner, we'll start a separate company but I still call the shots, you OK with that?"

"I'm all in and let me tell you why, since you disappeared for the past 2 weeks we've been busy over here tracking the movement of the mutant alloy and guess what, we found a way to modify one side of the molecule and it repels itself just like your test panel but that's not the best part" Phil went on "are you sitting down?"

"Yes" I said.

"Remember that extraneous energy source I mentioned after our first examination, well I had the boys from our space science division look at it and in their opinion the only possible answer is some kind of a Dark Energy reaction." I slumped back in my chair dumbfounded.

"Phil I thought Dark Energy was only a theory."

"It is, and this is the first real evidence of its existence, Nobel Prize stuff."

"Maybe" I said, "but remember the guys from the University of Penn that invented the transistor, they were awarded the Nobel Prize, divvied up a million bucks and got gold Rolex watches. 2 years later RCA, Sony and Texas Instruments to name a few began mass producing transistor radios, calculators and a thousand other products and made billions. This is a game changer Phil and I already have a Rolex."

Chapter 2

THE DREAM MACHINE

"Marie" I hollered, "get my accountant on the phone and try to find a retired air force colonel by the name of Tony Colby."

"Who?" she asked walking into my office.

"Anthony J Colby he's a friend, last known address was Fort Drum New York." Five minutes later Marie's voice came over the intercom.

"Mr. Campo is on line two."

"Joseph, how's our credit line doing?"

"You can still do McDonalds" he said laughing, "but I would stay away from the Trattorias."

"Joe I need to borrow 5 million bucks, if I put everything on the line is it doable?"

"Are you kidding I'm not a magician Tom."

"I mean it Joe, use all my personal and company assets, properties, bank accounts, IRA's the whole shooting match and yes you are a magician, see what you can come up with."

"You are serious, let me go over the statements, I'll make a few phone calls and get back to you."

Joe Campo was another classmate; after college he interned with a big 10 accounting firm and got his CPA. A rising star in the firm he earned millions for his clients and specialized in corporate finance and acquisitions. After a stint on Wall Street and several nasty divorces, he retired to private practice, operating a 5 man shop. I was always impressed with Joe's ability to structure a deal and get it financed. He was like a bloodhound once he had the scent you could be sure he would find it. As expected Joe was on the phone the next day.

"Tom, good morning got good and bad news, we may be able to get the money but I had to go to the secondary market and you know what that means."

"Yea I know scalper rates and points, any port in a storm though."

"I was able to get a commitment for half at conventional rates," Joe added, "but the second half will cost you."

"Let's do this, commit to the conventional line and we'll keep the 2nd line on ice until it's needed, can we do that?"

"Sure Tom, but if your statements keep going down-hill we can lose it."

"Understood", I replied, "let me know when I can start writing checks."

Joe and I came from the same neighborhood, an Italian inner city enclave known as South Philadelphia. Growing up amidst an immigrant and young working class families the bonds made as kids were durable lasting a lifetime. We lived in small 2 story row homes; if you had a 3 story home you were considered mobbed up or connected, the whole family shared a single bathroom and a rotary phone,

2 were considered a luxury. Our whole lives as kids revolved around a 3 or 4 square block area consisting of a catholic school and church, (public schools didn't count), a square (a cinder covered athletic field), the corner, usually a small neighborhood candy store or luncheonette where we met, hung out, and sang Doo-Wop; a neighborhood wine maker who sold Dago Red by the milk bottle, a homemade brew guaranteed to cure any ailment you had or thought you had and corner grocery stores that gave us most of what we ate from soup to nuts. The best part of that was nothing went bad, you could easily buy what you needed for a day or two and simply walk a block and buy some more, no traffic jams, parking problems or wasted time. It was an age of Rock and Roll singing groups, all home grown products and we all believed we were the next upcoming heart throb. During the summer if you were lucky, you spent weekends in Atlantic City or Wildwood and every morning we had street vendors in horse drawn wagons selling their wares. GEVELLA WATER, the Italian phrase for Clorox usually woke me by 7 AM. This was followed by fruit and produce vendors, milk men, egg men and even rag men - yep salesmen actually knocked on your door selling an assortment of rags (this part of business was usually controlled by Jewish merchants, along with clothing and shoe ware), the Italian merchants were too occupied with food to care.

Life was simpler then, you only needed to follow a few important rules and if broken punishment was quick and sure. This was our home, we knew who we were and believed there was nothing we couldn't do. Years later after going our separate ways I bumped into Joe at a Christmas party thrown by my attorney. I had finally settled a grueling divorce and in addition to being emotionally upset I felt a whole lot poorer. This particular divorce judge was ruthless, a female jurist with a major attitude against any and all husbands and as my attorney mentioned I was lucky to get away with my skin. It was good to see an old friend again and in that one chance meeting he reminded me where I came from, the optimism and confidence of my youth constantly reflected by family and neighbors; even if they didn't know your name you could see the approval in their faces as if to say we're counting on you kid, go out and make your way and let the world know where you came from. I had forgotten and it made me realize I needed to pick up the pieces and start over again. I never mentioned to Joe how much help he was just by being there but I promised myself I would find a way to return the favor one day.

It was getting late and I hung up and pressed the intercom, "Marie, I need you."

"Be right there" she replied. A few seconds later she pranced into my office, sat down by my desk and pulled her dress up high on her thighs, "OK what can I do for you" she purred while smiling. My brain went blank for a moment and I felt flushed, she zinged me I thought and I liked it.

"You keep that up and we'll never get out of here."

"I've got the time" she replied while leaning over my desk, her well-formed cleavage spreading out of her bra and I instinctively reached out and caressed her breast. I was on remote control now as I pulled her up pressing her hips to mine. Her eyes were begging as our lips hungrily ate at each other like wild dogs on a kill. A few minutes later we lay naked on my couch, spent and satisfied.

"Next time" I said, "we've got to take it slower, this feels too good to go so fast." Marie smiled and clung to me.

"It's been a while for me I'd almost forgotten," she shivered and moaned "let's do this again sometime." We lay there for about an hour and got dressed.

"Jesus, it's almost 7:30," I said, "don't you have kids to feed?"

"Not this week, my ex has them all to himself."

"Are you OK Marie?"

"Tom, I'm not a little girl, I've done this before, it was great but not a big deal."

"I know, I just don't want this to interfere with our working relationship and that is a big deal."

"Not to worry, see you in the morning" she added walking away.

On the way home I felt like a teenager and reminisced my early years, sweet bird of youth, I thought, how sweet it is. By the time I got to my Condo I was starving; I took off my coat, popped a frozen dinner into the microwave, opened a bottle of beer and watched the second half of a Phillies game. By 10 O'clock I was yawning and thought, this is the way it should always be; slept like a baby that night.

The next day I arrived at the office early. Marie wasn't there yet, and I put a pot of coffee on and went into my office reminiscing last night. I was staring out of my window watching rush hour traffic build when Marie walked in with a cup of coffee.

"Cream no sugar" she said putting the cup on my desk.

"Good, you're still alive", I laughed, "We've got a lot of work today."

"I've got a few things to take care of," Marie replied, "the new draftsman, Mark, you hired last month starts today and I want to get him oriented."

"OK, get him a desk and a phone and turn him over to one of the engineers, let him figure it out for himself." With that Marie left and all seemed normal, she was cool, no emotional baggage from last night, or at least she didn't show it.

We needed a better name for our repelling panel I thought, as Marie came back in.

"OK what are we doing today?" she asked.

"I want to start a new company Marie, set up the forms for an LLC, Phil Visi and myself will be the principles,"

"and the name is..?" she waited,"

"Don't know yet, but it's going to be a one product company for the repelling panel."

"You mean Einstein's Folly that Jim Dougherty calls it."

"One and the same" I said.

"Well why not name the company after the product?"

"We could except we already have lots of names for it."

"What does it do?"

"It propels itself" I said.

"You figure it out Tom, I'm sure there's some combination that works, try an acronym, in the meantime let me get started on the LLC…Oh by the way I found your Colonel Colby his phone number is in your email."

"Thanks Marie, I'll get you a name today." Marie's questions started me thinking of an acronym. The descriptors

I liked were Dark Energy, Anti-Gravity and Magic machine or DEAM….. Didn't sound right, using DR for dark or DREAM worked better and adding propelling or propulsion system; DREAM Propulsion Systems LLC – Good that was it, code name DREAM.

I sat back and grinned, good name I thought as I tracked down Tony Colby's phone number from the maze of unopened emails on my computer. The phone rang five times before I heard a raspy voice with an inpatient tone saying

"It's your dime talk," I started to laugh,

"Tony it's Tom D'Antonio, how the hell are you Colonel."

"Tom" his voice changed, "Tom is that you, you old bastard, I figured you'd be dead by now,"

"no still here in the flesh and blood, but thanks for the vote of confidence anyway."

"Well what have you been up to son?"

"Tony I'm working on an interesting program, very special and I could use your help. Can you spare some time and come see me; by your area code it looks like you're living in the DC area."

"Right you are boy, Alexandria, I had a heart problem several years ago and did a stint at Walter Reed for a few months, figured I stay around here in case anything else popped up."

"I didn't know Tony."

"Naw I'm fit as a fiddle now, no problem, anyway what's this special program you're babbling about?"

"You're only 2 hours away, look up my company ArmorTec. I'll fill you in on the details when you get here."

"You're on buddy, give me a few days to take care of things and I'm yours."

"Great, see you next week Tony" I smiled and hung up.

Tony Colby was an Iraq war Vet, and a career soldier. He entered the air force right out of college and retired 20 years later as a full Colonel. His specialty was communications and security, and in that roll had many high level contacts at the pentagon and the board rooms of the largest defense contractors. He turned down several lucrative positions in industry, to care for an ailing wife, but personally knew and was respected by everyone who was anybody in the defense industry, and it was just that asset that I needed now.

In his early years Tony walked around with a chip on his shoulder, always looking for a fight. I remembered his father saying the little bastard was born with a scowl on his face. I don't believe he had the slightest idea that his son was just like him and I didn't have the heart to tell him. By the time we graduated college, Tony already had several purple hearts from the scraps he got into so going into the military seemed a natural progression. He really wore his patriotism on his sleeve and proudly defended everything American, earning the nickname "Captain America," courtesy of the guys in our ROTC class. To this day I believe the Army turned him down as a section 8 but recommended him to an Air Force recruiter just for the hell of it. In any event the conflict in Viet Nam was drawing down as Tony was graduating officer candidate school and his true baptism of fire would have to wait for future conflicts in the Middle East. Age and a family has a way of mellowing most men and Tony was no different; only in his case military life brought out the leadership character of the man and by the end of his second tour of duty he became the youngest Lieutenant Colonel and ultimately full Bird Colonel since the early days of WW II. Only health problems held back his further advancement and his career path shifted into Asymmetric Warfare, hidden away deep in the secure recesses of the Pentagon.

The following day I got Phil Vizi back on the phone.

"Phil is there a way to duplicate the molecule you modified and commercially apply it on a panel."

"Tall order Tom, maybe some of the folks in Silicon Valley have an idea. They process computer chips by electronically plating molecular structures on silicon wafers, could be done if we can supply the molecules. Let me think about this and I'll get back to you." It's a start I thought, but we would still have to scale up the application to a useable size. We weren't going to compute anything; we needed to develop power and a whole lot of it.

Joe Campo had just hung up on an unexpected call. The Black Rock group was interested in financing ArmorTec and wanted to review its project portfolio. A senior account manager by the name of Jeff George said they represented a private investor that was interested in defense related programs. Joe was suspicious, they could have certainly learned of ArmorTec's financial condition, a matter of public record as a prime government contractor. They would have known the programs, everything he thought except for Hyper Jet, which did not require disclosure as a self-funded project. In any event Joe had agreed to meet with George to discuss ArmorTec's financial needs. Black Rock's offices where located in Washington DC, a short train ride for Joe from his Wilmington home. Walking into Black Rock's offices Joe was impressed with its posh ambiance located in the heart of DC close to the Reagan building. A Knockout blue eyed blonde greeted him as he waited in the lobby.

"Mr. Campo," she said, with a sexy southern drawl "welcome, my name is Lana, if you'll follow me I'll take you to the conference area." They walked down a long hall passed a dozen offices into a glass menagerie of a conference room. "Mr. George will be with you in a moment, can I get you something" she asked, "coffee, tea, water?" For a moment Joe stuttered.

"No I'm fine Lana, maybe later." With that she turned and walked to the door, looking back she pressed a switch and the floor to ceiling glass wall along the hall instantly became white opaque panes.

"For privacy" she smiled and closed the door.

A short time later a large ruddy faced individual came in.

"Hello Joe, welcome to Black Rock, I'm Jeff George," he bellowed. "Glad you could make it, I think you'll find it was well worth the trip." Without hesitating George continued on, "my client is interested in ArmorTec's product line and we are prepared to provide whatever financing you need, how's that sound?" he grinned. Joe smiled back.

"Great, if you'll just write a check I'll be on my way." George let out a loud nervous laugh and slapped his leg.

"Boy I knew I liked you the first time we talked, all we need is a standard plain language contract giving us a minority share of the company and a seat on the board and I can write that check, today if you want."

"Mr. George," George interrupted,

"Call me Jeff, why we're practically partners." Joe continued.

"Jeff, I only represent ArmorTec, I appreciate your directness but any proposal you offer would have to be approved by ArmorTec's board, I'm only here to see if there's a possible fit."

"Well hell boy I know that, I just want you to know we're rearing to go."

"Can you tell me a little more about this client you represent?"

"Sure Joe, but he's more like a silent partner with very deep pockets if you know what I mean" and added, "at Black Rock we pride ourselves in holding in strict confidence all of our clients principals, we're the operators and you would interface with those boys out in the hall."

"Why ArmorTec?" Joe asked.

"You guys are leading edge, that's the word we got from the Pentagon and at Block Rock we only deal with the best."

"Need to take back something more than that Jeff."

"Look Joe," Jeff began in a more serious tone, "we know you're looking for financing, this is a money deal, I've got five million bucks burning a hole in my pocket right now; we don't want to crimp your style just want to help you grow. You'll have to take my word on that for now. I'll leave a copy of the contract with you, if you like it you know where to find me."

Joe knew it was pointless to press any further.

"Fair enough Jeff" he said, while getting out of his chair, "Thanks for the offer, I'll see what I can do." Joe left the conference room and as he turned down the hall Lana walked up behind him and slipped her hand under his arm. "First class service," he said.

"Nothing but the best for a Black Rock customer" she replied, "are you staying in town tonight?"

"No I hadn't planned to." Lana paused with him in the lobby and handed him her card.

"Next time call, I'll take care of your reservation," she smiled and disappeared down the hall. Joe remained for a minute trying to decipher what that was all about. Walking out of the building he knew one thing, regardless if ArmorTec was going to do business with Black Rock he was coming back at least one more time.

Jeff George was rehashing the exchange with Joe Campo, when his secretary called.

"Mr. Bickford on line two."

"Hello Jack, Campo left a few minutes ago and I was just getting ready to call you."

"How did it go?" Bickford asked.

"I think OK, he wanted to know who's putting the money up and why, told him ArmorTec had the reputation."

"Listen Jeff I know D'Antonio he'll never buy that bullshit, push Campo, get him some incentive to sell our deal and get your alternate plan ready in case that fails."

"I'm already dangling incentive under Campo's nose Jack, we'll make it happen."

"Hello Tom I'm on the train from Washington, thought I give you a heads up on my meeting with Black Rock while it's still fresh in my head."

"Sure Joe go ahead, I'm all ears." Joe finished relating his conversation with Jeff George and asked,

"What do you think, it'll solve a lot of problems for us and maybe add some new resources we could use."

"Like what?" I asked.

"Well for starters Black Rock ain't no slouch, they have a lot of clout and could be a great intro into other areas."

"Joe," I interrupted, "our main focus and maybe our only focus right now is the magic alloy, besides this really sounds over the top, dig deeper, I'm not about to get in bed with an unknown silent partner despite Black Rock's reputation." I looked up and saw Phil Visi waiting in the lobby, "got to go Joe, let me know when you come up with something."

Phil walked into my office smiling from ear to ear.

"Found the switch" he announced, "the on-off switch for the magic molecule."

"What the hell are you talking about?" I asked.

"The dark energy reaction" Phil stammered, "I found a way to turn it on and off. Remember the electron cloud I told you we saw around the first target samples, well it turns out that a very specific electrical input to the molecule disrupts the cloud and turns off the dark energy reaction. Remove the input and the reaction comes right back."

"Unbelievable Phil, this just keeps on getting better and better, now if you can find a way to produce them we may have something."

"May be closer than you think Tom, my contacts in Silicon Valley put me onto a small R&D firm in Cambridge that specializes in growing crystals."

"Growing crystals" I interrupted in surprise, "growing crystals?"

"Oh yea, I forgot to mention the other anomaly we uncovered, our magic molecule also exhibits crystalline properties, really strange, but it also means that we may be able to grow it like a pure monolithic structure. The Cambridge firm developed a process using an atomic absorption scaffold that can be seeded with a molecule and shazam, it populates the entire scaffold - pretty neat han, they call it "Crystalline Absorption Scaffolding Technology" or CAST which is exactly what it does. If we can grow or cast blocks of our molecule we can slice it into useable tiles and apply them like the insulation tiles NASA used on the space shuttle."

"My God Phil you know this will work?"

"Not yet Tom, I'm going up there tomorrow to set up a test, if we can prove it in the lab the process is scalable and we'll be able to produce in quantity."

"Look Phil, we need to keep the genie in the bottle; don't let anyone outside of ArmorTec know the details. I'm getting vibes that some folks in the defense community already have an idea."

"Understood" Phil replied, "I've already thought of a diversion and I can mask the energy effect if needed." As Phil left the office I began to realize the full scope of the undertaking we had embarked on and the depth of resources that would be needed; far more than I had originally foreseen.

I heard a familiar voice and laughter coming from the lobby; it was Tony Colby referring to me as his long lost cousin.

Marie turned her head towards me with an amused look. I nodded and waved to send him in.

"Tony" I said while standing up, "glad you made it buddy, sit down and let me tell you what were up to." An hour later Tony looked perplexed,

"Tom, if this is real you can't keep it a secret, My God, you have an obligation for the good of the country."

"Don't want to keep it a secret Tony, just want to move it further down the road and get some control. If I let it out now you know those power hungry whores in Washington will find a way to screw me and justify it for the good of the country. They'll use Eminent Domain as an excuse and that's what I'm afraid of."

"You've got a point but it seems to me there is a way for you to be a player and do the right thing; classic case of cellar technology."

"What technology?" I asked, Tony continued.

"The Wright brothers developed the first and best real flying machine at the time. They also tried to exclude using anybody else's innovations and refused to play ball with mainstream players including the US Air Force, so what happened next?… guys like Jack Northrop and Sam Langley managed to reinvent the best features of the Wright brothers design, adopted other improvements including new, more powerful Allison engines and created an aviation industry. In other words they pushed the technology out of the cellar. The rest is history, the fledgling industry fueled by a World War took off; eventually went to the moon and the Wright brothers were relegated to a footnote in history."

"Quaint story Tony, how does that help me?"

"You need a White Knight" he replied, "somebody that has enough money and horsepower to dig in and push back. If you can't beat them, you know the rest, the name of the game is speed, staying ahead of the pack."

"Working on that as we speak" I said, "but still looking for the right option, what do you know about Black Rock?"

"Not a whole lot, as I recall they keep their activities very confidential but I do know some of the Lobbyist they work with, you know the beltway bandits, they'd sell their mothers for a buck. Let me see what I can find out, I assume you mean their sudden interest in ArmorTec."

"Yep, particularly the silent partner that's interested; you can work out of here when you're in town Tony, Marie will set you up with an office. How's special projects director sound for a title?"

"I don't give a damn what you call me, head janitor for all I care, what's the pay?"

"You'll get exactly what you deserve," I replied laughing. Tony was a good egg, I thought, someone I could trust and confide in, someone who would watch my back.

One week had passed since Joe Campo visited Black Rock and couldn't shake any information loose regarding their operations or funding sources. Time to go direct, he thought and the only insider he knew besides Jeff George was Lana.

"Good afternoon Lana its Joe Campo," he said over the phone.

"Mr. Campo, what a pleasant surprise, what can I do for you?"

"I'm scheduled to be in Washington tomorrow and wanted to see if you're available for dinner, you were so hospitable on my last visit I'd like to show my gratitude."

"Nonsense Mr. Campo you don't owe me anything and yes I'd love to meet you for dinner, just tell me where and when."

"Lana please call me Joe, there's a Hilton close to your office on south west 26th Street. They have an excellent restaurant, why don't I meet you in the bar say about 6:30."

"I know the place, it is very good, see you then, and Joe….. I'm very glad you called," she added in a slow accentuated southern drawl.

Joe arrived at union station at 6:15 and 20 minutes later at the Hilton hoping Lana would be waiting in the bar. Not here yet, he thought, quickly scanning the room as he sat at the bar and ordered a drink. Another 15 minutes passed and he began to feel edgy wondering if Lana would show, as she walked up behind him.

"Sorry I'm late Joe, some last minute issues at the office, couldn't be helped."

"Know the feeling," Joe replied while giving her a friendly hug, "don't give it another thought I'm already one drink ahead of you."

Dinner and a bottle of wine later they passed the evening casually talking about their lives and work. Lana was in her mid-thirties and haled from Savannah Georgia. Married right out of college her ambition led her to pursue an opening in DC as a congressional aide and with the help of a family contact was soon working for Senator Gingrich as a policy assistant. Her marriage didn't last and 4 years later left the hill to work for Black Rock.

"Lana, I hope you don't mind talking shop, has Black Rock always been so secretive about their activities?"

"Only until they get to know you better, you realize how nasty this town can be."

"Oh I'm aware," he said, "but it's hard to cut a deal without knowing who you're involved with." Lana smiled,

"let's not get ahead of ourselves Joe, first things first and that's desert at my place." Without a word Joe quickly paid the tab, Lana took him by the hand and they walked out the door.

Her apartment was in a swanky part of town not far from the Watergate complex.

"Want a drink?" she asked.

"Yea, I'll have a night cap."

"The bars next to the kitchen, make me one too while I get changed."

Joe was trying to focus on his mission but his brain was getting wild with anticipation. Lana soon came out of her bedroom dressed in a lacey jump suit that accentuated her exquisite female curves.

"That's better" she said, as she curled up next to him on the couch. Joe's hormones were now getting the better of him and in a daze he leaned over and touched her face watching her fleshy red lips move apart. She moaned as his hand slid up her uncovered thighs and moved to the bedroom franticly peeling their clothes off. A short time later laying there satisfied and out of breath Lana smiled and said, "I know why you came here Joe, I want to help you make this deal if I can." Surprised at her directness Joe felt a little embarrassed,

"after tonight, you are my deal," he whispered while pulling her body close to his; "I'm not sure I care about anything else."

All the pieces were starting to come together. Phil Visi confirmed the CAST process worked at Cambridge and we now had a way to produce power panels. Our bank loan was in place and I still had the offer from Black Rock to consider. The pleasant contemplations of the day were suddenly shattered by a phone call from Jim Dougherty.
"Mr. D, we had a break in at the range last night, I found one of our techs this morning. He was badly beaten, the ambulance just left."

"Christ Jim how bad was he hurt?"

"Not sure, looked like he was cut up pretty bad, he was barely conscious when I found him. He did mumble something about Einstein's Folly, his words not mine."

"Whoa, back up Jim," I hollered, "is the panel still there?"

"Yes it is, I had it moved to a shed in back of the north range for security purposes, no one else knew about it."

"Good man," I said, relieved, "meet me at the hospital I want to make sure our guy's taken care of."

Walking into the emergency entrance at Cooper hospital we quickly located our range tech, Charlie Kryzwiki, in one of the bays of the trauma unit.

"How's he doing?" I asked one of the attending physicians.

"He has a couple of broken ribs and severe lacerations. We managed to stop the bleeding, other than that he'll be OK with some rest."

"Thanks Doc, can I talk to him for a minute?"

"Only a minute, I've given him a sedative and don't want him to get excited."

"Charlie looked bad, black and blue with stitched gashes on his chin and forehead, in a low voice I asked, "how you doing buddy?" His eyes opened and he moaned in a barely auditable tone.

"Been better, Doc says I'll survive."

"Can you tell me who did this?"

"Couple of guys, three I think, broke thru the gate and came screeching up to the bunker in a black Van. Before I knew it one of them pinned me on the ground and shouted tell me where the test panel is. I shoved him off and jumped up then the other two did a job on me. Very professional, they knew what they were doing, karate kicks, chops, not typical thugs. They asked me again, only this time for the Hyper Jet test panel. I grabbed one of them and spit in his face, then everything went black, that's all I remember."

"Thanks Charlie get some rest, we'll get the bastards," turning to leave Charlie added,

"Oh one more thing, I did manage to rip off a tag or logo on one of their shirts, must have dropped it after I went out."

Outside the ER, Jim turned to me with a menacing look, something I had not seen before.

"The bastards are not going to get away with this, Charlie was one of my guys his safety was my responsibility."

"Jim, the best thing you can do right now is search the site where you found Charlie this morning, any evidence we can recover will help in the police investigation."

"Yea I'll do that too but I promise you there won't be anything left if I get my hands on them first."

"Let the police handle it," I said… Jim looked away from me and nodded. As he drove off, I had the impression he neither heard what I said, or cared.

My cell phone rang, it was Marie.

"Hello Tom, how's Charlie?"

"He'll be alright, looks worse than it is."

"Thank God," she replied.

"Listen Marie, I need you to call, Phil Visi and Joe Campo, tell them to be at the office first thing tomorrow morning, its important; is Tony still there?"

"Yes, he just stepped out to get some lunch."

"Good make sure he's there to," I said.

"Oh by the way Jim Dougherty called, he's taking a few days off, something about a family matter, any idea what that's about?"

"Damn-it…….maybe, I'm not sure." Jim had a dark side, I thought, a very powerful dark side and I was afraid it was about to get out of control.

The next day Phil, Joe and Tony were sitting in the conference room when I got to the office.

"Glad you're all here, we need to step things up a notch and speed up the DREAM project, kick it in the ass. We've got to have a full plan, soup to nuts, more resources and product, lots of it."

"Hold on Tom where you going with this," Tony asked.

"I don't know, out of this world," I said halfheartedly, "maybe Mars." Phil laughed,

"Sure and maybe we can go back in time and visit our dead relatives."

"Look, we've got a big product" I went on, "and it needs a big idea. If we don't do it someone else will and I'm sure there are people out there already gunning for us."

"You're forgetting one thing," Joe cut in, "big ideas need big money, a hell of a lot more than we have or could borrow, where you going to get it?"

"Phil you rub shoulders with all those internet billionaires, especially the rocket junkies looking to commercialize space travel. Tony you have contacts in Washington with enough money to rebuild New York City for Christ sakes, let's use them. We have the dough to build a working model, a demonstrator power panel and we can do that now, right!"…

"Yes we can," Phil agreed, "I already have a molecular prototype, it wouldn't be a big deal to scale it up, and I think I know just the guy who would flip over this"….

"Yea and I know a few financial heavyweights, looking for deep projects" Tony added, "and they'd be glad to stay on the sidelines and watch our backs, maybe even get the Government to help out."

"OK, let's start today, get Marie a list of everything you need, including a budget and work the program."

"Tom we still need a plan, what's the end game?" Joe asked.

"Why not Mars, it's certainly big enough and it'll capture the public's imagination…. news men would have a field day with it."

After the meeting I asked Joe to see me in my office.

"Joe close the door, I want to keep this confidential, you know what happened last night at our test range."

"Yea it's terrible, lots of crazy people out there."

"Well what you don't know is that they were after the Hyper Jet test panel and they were professionals, maybe paramilitary." Joe went pale and slid back in his chair.

"Jesus Christ, are you thinking what I'm thinking?"

"Yes I am but I have to know for sure, you've got to get me some Intel on Black Rock. We have to know what we're dealing with, If my hunch is right, things are about to get ugly."

Chapter 3
A WAY TO GO

The Mars project was moving into high gear. A few weeks had passed and our power panel demonstrator was completed, evidencing an energy density of 10 pounds per cubic inch. The, 6" x 12," panel with its disrupter switch engaged, weighed in at 18 pounds of diamond hard material; with the switch off, the full effect of the dark energy reaction pushed the panel weight to a staggering 2,160 pounds.

Phil Visi had convinced one of his internet buddies to take a look at our DREAM propulsion system. Robert Tosky was a visionary, the oldest son of Lithuanian immigrants; his father worked in the stock yards of Chicago saving every possible dime to ensure his children were well educated. After graduating from Princeton, along with a few school buddies, he formed an internet start-up in the early 90's, just as the industry was starting to explode. He was one of the first to recognize that the software model, dominated by Microsoft, was not where the technology was headed; anticipating this paradigm shift, made him a fortune selling his cloud-computing services company.

Shortly after, he acquired one of NASA's vehicle development companies, competing with the Russian Soyuz 6 program. Alpha Vehicles occupied a strategic nitch having successfully developed small, near space prototype vehicles that had been put on the back burner by NASA due to funding cut backs and Tosky was determined to take advantage of the situation. The Government was playing hardball these days, and you needed capital to stay in the game. Tosky understood this and bought out Alpha at a deep discount, keeping its management team and intellectual property in place. With a healthy influx of cash and Tosky at the helm, the company quickly got back on track and was now pitching NASA for a service contract using its most recent version of a resupply vehicle for the International Space Station.

Jim Dougherty pulled up to a townhouse in Georgetown with a black van parked in the driveway. A torn Black Rock logo lay on his seat that he found at the range; every day for a week he sat outside Black Rock's offices until the van he followed to Georgetown parked outside; following the two well-dressed men from the van into the building, they waved at the receptionist and disappeared down a hall. The receptionist looked at Jim and said,

"Can I help you?"

"I thought I recognized one of the men that just went by, old service buddy, you wouldn't know his name?"

"Oh, you must mean Bryan Adams, I believe he was in the military."

"No my mistake, looks just like my friend though, sorry" Jim replied and quickly left the building.

Jim checked his pistol, placed it in his shoulder harness hidden under his coat and knocked on the door.

"Hello, I'm from the Wounded Warrior's Foundation looking for Bryan Adams,"

"That's me what's this about."

"Bryan, if I could have a minute of your time, I'll explain an urgent matter that's extremely important to all service members."

"OK, come on in, don't have much time, I'm a little busy today."

"John Parker," Jim said extending his hand, "special forces, captain, retired." After a brief cordial conversation, Adams mentioned that he left the service and was working for an executive security firm, the profile fit Jim thought. Adams got up and said,

"I really have to go."

"One more thing, ever hear of a firm called ArmorTec?" Jim asked sternly, Adams face turned red and his eyes opened wide,

"No, no, don't think so, why do you ask?" he stuttered.

"Hyper Jet ring a bell," Jim snapped. Adams backed up with a panic look on his face.

"GET OUT" he shouted, reaching for Jim's arm… Jim instinctively caught his hand and swept him to the floor with a leg kick in one motion while pulling his pistol out with his free hand.

"Listen to me real good, you worthless piece of shit, if you tell me what I need to know I may let you live." Adams stared back wild eyed and yelled,

"Fuck you, I'm not telling you anything."

"OK" Jim said calmly, and pulled the trigger putting a slug into his leg.

"Wait a minute, WAIT A MINUTE," he screamed, "I was only the driver."

"You get one more chance at this you miserable lowlife" Jim said and proceeded with his interrogation. His story made sense,

"now call an ambulance I'm bleeding to death," Adams pleaded.

"Yea, just like you did for Charlie, if you lied to me, I swear, I'll come back and kill you."

"I told you everything I know," he sobbed, "now call the ambulance, please, please." Jim's rage was uncontrollable; leaning over him he put a deep gash in his forehead with the butt of his pistol.

"Call your own ambulance scumbag, now you look like Charlie."

"Mr. Tosky and Phil Visi are here," Marie's voice echoed over the intercom. Walking into my office, Bob Tosky was a tall slender man with a confident, friendly manner I surmised, wondering if that was only his work persona.

"Hello Bob," I said shaking his hand, "nice to finally meet you, Phil's told me a lot about you."

"All good stuff I hope," Tosky grinned, "Phil's one of the finest bull-shitters I know." A few minutes later with the chatter out of the way, I asked,

"What do you think of our propulsion system?"

"Hard to believe, Tom, but if the good doctor Visi says it's so, I believe, where do you think you want to go with this?"

"To Mars" I said, he smiled, "I'm dead serious," I added.

"Ambitious venture," he replied, "do you have any idea what that would cost and the resources and facilities you'd need?"

"We have a plan… look Bob, I realize the scope of the project, I also know it's not a one company deal, certainly not ArmorTec anyway. I figure if we can get it going with the technology we have it'll attract the necessary resources, even Government help."

"A bit naïve, don't you think," Tosky asked, "for one thing, you'll never be able to get a rocket off the ground without Government approval and I can assure you, the big boys in the backroom of the aerospace industry won't let that happen."

"Thought of that to, I want you to meet a close friend of mine…. Marie," I called on the intercom, "ask Tony to come in."

"Colonel Colby, say hello to Bob Tosky," I said.

"Heard about you Bob, you coming to Mars with us too?" he asked, we all laughed, it broke the tension that was building.

"Sure, I'll buy a ticket, but before we go you have to convince me that I won't get killed in a launch pad explosion or deported for violating FAA regulations."

"Bob, I spent a career manipulating political decisions for the Pentagon in the bowels of Capitol Hill, after all the bullshit, two timing, and horse trading deals, one thing I've come to realize is that our institutions still work for the good of the country. If you really have something and make them understand you can prevail, but we have to be prepared, must have the horsepower to get it done, I think that's why you're here today." Tony was on a roll, I thought, Tosky was impressed, although he probably needed more assurance that he wouldn't be throwing a good chunk of his fortune down the toilet. We needed a more compelling argument.

The next day Jim Dougherty showed up at the office.
"Where the hell have you been?" I asked.
"Long story Mr. D," he said and began, relating his episode at Black Rock and with Bryan Adams. "The bastards were setting us up and not on their own."
"Maybe," I replied,
"I believed Adams," he said,
"How can you be sure?"
"Because I've seen this before, when the human body is in that much pain and you're scared to death, you tell the truth, it's not a choice, but he couldn't tell me who's pulling Black Rock's strings, all he knew was that they're from one of the big aerospace firms, his orders came directly from a guy named George at Black Rock." The name rang a bell.
"Good work Jim, why don't you take a few more days off."
"No way Mr. D, I want to get back to my crew and tighten up security procedures, this isn't going to happen again." Jim left and I pressed the intercom,
"Marie, track down Joe Campo and tell him to call the office, high priority." I was sure Joe had mentioned a George, Jeff George, I recalled… if Jim's story held up I knew this wouldn't stop, we needed to find a smoking gun and we needed it soon.

Marie's voice came over the intercom,

"Campo's on line two Tom."

"Joe, Jim Dougherty showed up today, he's been AWOL for the past week," I continued, relaying Jim's story.

"I was afraid this might happen, when Black Rock finds out they'll circle the wagons," Joe said, "now what the hell do we do?"

"For starters, who are the Aerospace firms dealing with Black Rock, their contracts must be a matter of public record, George though, he's the key, I'd give my right arm for a copy of his telephone log." Joe hesitated.

"Maybe we can do better than that."

"Yea, like what," I asked.

"Have to run, I'll get back to you," he said, and hung up.

Later that week Phil Visi walked into my office with a determined look.

"Tosky's definitely interested, after our meeting he insisted on having dinner, wanted to know if Mars was for real and would you be open to a counter offer."

"That's something anyway, better than I expected, what was the counter offer?"

"Never gave him a chance to propose anything, told him Mars was not negotiable, I figured now is not the time for quibbling; he's the kind of guy that likes team players that believe, if we're not convinced why should he be."

"Would have been nice to find out if he's a buyer," I interrupted, "but I like your thinking, go on."

"I spent 3 hours going over our plan in detail, including financials, he knows the power panel is a world beater but he's thinking about all the other on earth commercial applications."

"They'll come later" I said impatiently, "but right now its Control, if we can't make our mark where nobody else is, sure as hell we'll lose it. Does he really think that company's like Boeing, GM, NASA for Christ's sake, will simply let him take over their turf?"

"Tom, let me finish, he knows that too. He also thinks our plan is doable, we just need a little more skin in the game and I think he's in."

Tony Colby was busy surveying the Washington landscape, like a master Architect, trying to put the pieces in place to satisfy the maze of regulatory and facility issues needed just to leave the planet. These were represented by neat little tag line boxes illustrated on the Gant chart of our Martian master plan, I'd have to call in a lot of favors, he was thinking, when his cell phone rang,

"Good morning Tony its Joe,"

"Well hello Mr. Campo where the hell have you been, could use some assistance around here if you're not too busy."

"Tony write this name down, Jack Bickford, got that?"

"Yea I got it so what."

"Can't go into it right now, just try to find out if he's connected with any of the large aerospace firms that are working with Black Rock, could you do that, and get back to me, it's important."

"Sure Joe, give me a day or two." Joe's tone of voice was disconcerting, he sounded scared and reading between the lines Tony was becoming worried he was getting into something over his head.

Lana's apartment was bathed in light in the midday sun. Joe Campo had been spending his weekends there and their one night business encounter was quickly turning into a full blown love affair. Joe had asked Lana for her help to find out who the silent partner was that was interested in ArmorTec, and Lana innocently complied. A list of outside associates that Jeff George regularly communicated with was obtained with the help of his secretary and a little investigation quickly narrowed the choices down to the name Jack Bickford. Joe walked up behind Lana, and put his arms around her waist.

"Honey I want you to be careful, make sure no-one can tie you into this, Black Rock is not going to appreciate you sharing their client names, especially silent partners, if they even suspect you could lose your job."

"And maybe I'll get promoted if this helps to close a deal with ArmorTec, besides if I get canned I can spend all my time with you," she laughed.

"I'm serious Lana, things could get dicey, ArmorTec may pass on this, and I just don't want your name to pop up."

Mike O'Brien was a retired CIA agent that made a living in the espionage industry. Information was his stock in trade which he plied ruthlessly in the embassy's surrounding Washington DC. Government agencies regularly used him to avoid any embarrassing indiscretions in foreign affairs, and they didn't particularly care how he got the job done. He was also a close friend of Tony Colby who pulled his ass out of a covert operation gone awry in Iraq.

"Tony its Mike," he said over his cell, "Jack Bickford is a regional manager at Atlas Industries; they're one of the largest Rocket manufacturers in the country and a major client of Black Rock."

"What else Mike, what about his profile, past activities, associations?"

"Nothing really bad except he's bounced around the industry for a long time, my gut tells me he's an ambitious wanna be that never made it to the top. One piece of information I recovered though you may be interested in, he was indicted as a co-conspirator along with several mob guys accused of attempted embezzlement. The charges didn't stick and the DA dropped the case; his attorney was able to have it expunged after the dust settled."

"Thanks Mike that tells me a lot, one more thing you can do for me,"

"Anything buddy, just name it."

"Need you to watch someone's back."

Our Mars plan was quickly filling in the gaps and becoming a reality at least on paper. A prototype ship design was laid out in three parts, a cargo section, crew quarters and a flight command module. Based on initial calculations, an estimated 1 million pounds of cargo and a ship weighing in at just under 450,000 pounds could be easily accelerated by the power panels.

First Stage Cargo Section

The first and largest stage, the Cargo section measured 40 feet in diameter standing 30 feet high. Given the power available, there was no need to utilize expensive light weight metals or composites – a simple stainless steel cylindrical structure with a 1 inch web would provide more than enough strength to securely carry heavy equipment and resist any micro meteor showers that may be encountered en-route. A mezzanine level at a height of 14 feet extended out 8 feet from the sidewall around the circumference; it would serve as additional storage space for provisions and an access way for securing and inspecting cargo components. The ship was designed so that each stage could be assembled on the launch pad and contained inter connecting structures on the top and bottom of each forward section. As the first part to touch down it was planned to disconnect and release the cargo section as a stand- alone structure, once on site it would serve as permanent quarters for the astronauts after off-loading the cargo. On the underside 4 large self-leveling pedestals were located to adjust for any ground irregularities on touch-down. An air lock and large aircraft type doors, providing a 12 by 12 foot access way, differentiating one side between 2 of the leveling pedestals. Along the outside circumference, 2 by 2 foot openings were cut into the sidewall, sealed on the inside with 1 inch thick bullet proof glass, and covered on the outside with a removable protective metal panel. These would serve as windows for each planned living quarters providing the habitat's occupants with sunlight and a panoramic Martian view.

Hybrid Vehicle

On the main cargo floor lock down stations were laid out to secure hybrid, hydrogen-electric powered equipment including, 2 small vehicles, and a variety of earth moving equipment. A self-contained solid state laboratory and one drill rig, extension rods and flow piping sufficient to tap 2,000 feet into an ice pack. A small nuclear powered generator capable of perpetually supplying enough electricity to maintain housing, ship and equipment services; once water flow from the ice pack was obtained, electrolysis operations, generating oxygen and hydrogen, would be pumped into pressure reservoirs. The oxygen, then piped to the crews quarters and ship to maintain a habitable environment, and the hydrogen now available would be the primary energy source for the hybrid fuel cell powered equipment.

These were the main cargo components in addition to a wide assortment of smaller equipment to fit out a machine shop, including a fully equipped tool crib. Stored on the mezzanine, were provisions to last an 8 man crew for an entire year; mainly an assortment of prepackaged NASA type meals color coded for breakfast, lunch and dinner. Individual living quarters for the permanent habitat, consisting of panelized knocked down modular units; each fully equipped containing bedding, zero gravity bath room, lighting, climate controls and a computer/communication work station. Utility hook ups were stubbed into the cargo floor at each planned location, to receive external plumbing and power after reassembling on site.

The total cargo weight came in at just over 800,000 pounds still well under the maximum design load for the ship. An ambitious mission plan, driven by the capabilities inherent in the power panels, set out not only to land on Mars but to establish the foundation for a permanent base to be revisited many times for years to come.

Dream Machine In Flight

The second stage sitting atop the cargo section is the ship's crew quarters and living facilities. A tapered cylindrical structure, measuring 40 feet at its base, 25 feet at its top, and rising 20 feet high. Inside the structure, 8 individual crew quarters similar to the units designed for the permanent habitat are positioned along the walls. The balance of the space, centrally located, contains, commissary and exercise facilities, and an open conference area with a large overhead LED screen for earth based video conferencing and exterior views provided by the recording equipment in the command module.

The DREAM propulsion system consisting of 4 power panels are attached to the midsection of this stage, each measuring 12 feet by 6 feet, 6 inches thick, and having an energy density of 10 pounds per cubic inch, capable of generating a propelling force in excess of 2 ½ million pounds. In the closed or vertical position, the panels are neutral exerting no lift; hinged to the walls at the top the free end rotates thru 90 degrees, to the horizontal position for maximum thrust. A reinforced hydraulic piston arm connected to the panel below its midsection precisely controls its rotation at any angle within the 90 degree arc, regulating panel thrust throughout its full range. Attitude control is similarly managed by varying the rotation of each individual panel at different angles; once the change in orientation is achieved the panels relocate to equivalent thrust positions to maintain the selected course.

The third and final stage, permanently attached to the top of the crew's quarters, is the command and control module, a bullet shaped structure measuring 15 feet in diameter and 18 feet in length. The top portion, an 8 foot high nose cone contains a maze of sensors, photographic and radar equipment, providing navigational awareness. A computerized control station occupies the main deck, monitoring all of the ships performance criteria, including component operating and maintenance status and trip log progress. A separate pilot's console, similar to the cockpit of a high performance aircraft, controls the DREAM propulsion system; speed, acceleration, steering and guidance instantly respond to the pilot's fingertip manipulation of a 3 axial joystick. The computerized fly by wire feature, in manual mode is a redundancy available for flight adjustments particularly prevalent for landing or emergency responses; this In addition to the way point navigation via automatic pilot mode, the primary flight control system.

Joe and Lana had just finished dinner and were walking back to Lana's apartment a few blocks away. The rays of the full moon gave an eerie glow to the ornate building details that lined the avenue. It was a cool summer night, rare for the DC climate, a soothing whispering breeze gave an aura of contentment, that all was right with the world. Turning the corner up an empty street, Joe never noticed the two men quickly approaching until they were 10 feet away. Looking up in alarm, he instinctively pulled Lana behind him as the two men confronted the couple.

"You two need to come with us Mr. Campo," a short stocky man said in a demanding voice.

"Who the hell are you and how do you know my name?" Joe stammered. With that the second man showed a pistol from under his coat and pushed Joe and Lana to the curb where a van had just pulled up.

"Get in now," he growled, "and no one will get hurt," stunned and shaken they reluctantly complied. As the van sped off Joe questioned the stocky man sitting next to Lana.

"This must be a mistake, where are you taking us and what do you want?"

"All your questions will be answered Mr. Campo, just sit back and this will be over soon." Stopped at a red light, a car speeding down a cross street, swerved and hit the front of the van blocking its path; the driver, wobbling, got out apparently drunk and stumbled over to the van, "I'm awfully sorry mister, guess I couldn't make that turn, is everybody all right," he slurred, while suspiciously scanning the contents of our van.

"Move that piece of shit you moron, before I get out and move it for you," our driver yelled.

"No, no please mister I'm sick you've got to help me," he yelled back, falling to his knees. Our stocky guard immediately got out, instructing the driver.

"Hurry, move his car and I'll take care of this bozo." In an instant the drunken bozo landed a hard punch to Mr. Stocky's groin and quickly disabled our driver slamming the car door on and breaking his outstretched arm. At the same time a second man in the car had crept over to the passenger side of our van unnoticed in the excitement and pressed a pistol against our gun totting abductor's head.

"Don't move don't even breathe meat head or your brains will be all over the dash" and looking back at us asked, "are you OK Mr. Campo?"

"Fine now,"

"Good," he replied, "give us a minute to take care of these clowns and we'll drive you back to your apartment," and snapping his wrist, he slammed his gun butt against our abductor's head knocking him cold. Mr. Stocky was still groveling on the ground as Mr. Bozo grabbed him by the throat.

"Listen my fat friend, if we weren't on a public street I'd put a bullet between your eyes right now. I know who you are and if anything happens to Mr. Campo, if he gets hit by a car, slips on a banana peel, anything, I'll track you down like a dog." Walking away he kicked in the side of Mr. Stocky's ribs, saying "that'll give you some down time to think about it." Driving back to Lana's apartment Joe said,

"Thanks for saving our asses, but who the hell are you?"

"Why we're the good guys Mr. Campo, compliments of Colonel Colby."

Driving over to Bob Tosky's office, the thought of a major international company like Atlas Rocket playing hard ball at our level was disconcerting. Even worse engaging in kidnapping and who knows what else if Colby's guy hadn't stepped in. Joe was shaken when he called and wanted to know how we were going to handle this, he was ready to walk, I thought at the time but also needed to know, for Lana's sake, this would not happen again. It took some convincing but Tony was able to calm him down assuring him that at least he would have a guardian angel until this was settled.

Tosky greeted me as I walked into his office.

"Thanks for coming over Tom, I wanted to continue our conversation about DREAM and felt it was important to do it in person."

"Feel the same way Bob, nothing like clearing the air in person, takes all the variables out of the equation." Tosky went on in detail about his ideas for transportation systems around the globe and the fortune that would result. When he was done he looked at me and said,

"I know you have concerns about the big boys taking over, Visi conveyed that to me but I can guarantee you that we would retain a major position no matter how the pie gets sliced and dealing with the transportation moguls of the world would only make it happen bigger and faster."

"Normally I would agree with that, conventional wisdom, text book stuff, but the likes of DREAM, has never happened before, you'd have to go back to the invention of the wheel, fire even for the kind of impact this holds for civilization."

"You're making my point," Bob replied, "we'll need the resources of civilization before this is over, a hell of a lot more than I have. We have the opportunity to change the world right now and for the better."

"I want to do that to, but in a measured way.....what do you think would happen if we offered DREAM up to the highest bidder... In my opinion chaos; look at oil or nuclear power for Christ Sakes, the world has already gone to war many times over such commodities, and DREAM can make them look like chump change."

"Sounds a little altruistic Tom, what are you afraid of?"

"I'll tell you what I'm afraid of, once we're into it regardless who we partner with, worldwide competition and the pace of technology will be so intense that we'll get trampled under and if we try to disrupt the billions in cash flow from those industries and antiquate thousands of factories, we'll never live to see the fortune you're talking about."

"Oh come on now," Tosky replied dismissively, "you don't really believe corporate America will be sending hit squads out for us, do you?"

"That's exactly what I'm saying, and guess what its already happening." Tosky sat back in his chair surprised at the assertion. I went on and explained the Black Rock – Atlas Rocket connection and the incidents at our range and in DC. When I was finished Tosky's face was pale,

"Christ I know those guys, I golf with some of the Atlas exec's, are you sure about this?"

"Bob I have the hospital bills and the police reports to prove it, we're just lucky that no one's been killed yet."

Bob Tosky arrived home late in the day, still startled at the revelations of the afternoon.

"I'm home," he called out walking in, "are we eating in or going out tonight," he asked, looking for his wife.

"Not tonight," she replied from somewhere in the kitchen, "I had a late brunch this afternoon, only feel like picking tonight, how about Chinese?"

"Sounds good, how was brunch?"

"Interesting, I hear you're going to Mars," she replied in a sarcastic tone. He was silent for a moment and a frown came over his forehead, he had always kept his wife informed of his business ventures as a polite gesture to their relationship, and Sylvia had always been supportive and why not, the results were great and she had a nearly unlimited spending budget, however his intuition was telling him this sounded different.

"Who told you that?" he asked, more a demand than a question.

"I had lunch with Sandy Visi today."

Sylvia and Sandy Visi were friends long before their husbands knew each other. They were sorority sisters at Penn but never very close. The two women didn't see each other for years until they met at an alumni luncheon in Philadelphia and continued to stay in touch through lunches once in a while. But today's luncheon was different, when Sandy called she sounded almost frantic. She asked Sylvia to meet her in the dining room at the Art Museum with an almost begging voice. It didn't matter what Sylvia had on her calendar, she knew that lunch with Sandy was a priority.

"What's the urgency?" Sylvia asked. Sandy carefully and slowly told Sylvia what Phil had confided in her. She explained as well as she could what the plans were at ArmorTec. Most of what she heard she didn't quite understand but the one thing she did understand was that they were planning to go to Mars and Bob Tosky was financing the venture to the tune of 10 billion dollars. "MARS, MARS," Sylvia choked out," Steven Spielberg goes to Mars on Warner Brothers back lot, everyone else goes to Europe." Sandy laughed out loud at Sylvia's reaction but assured her that this wild scheme was in the works; "and what do you mean 10 billion dollars, who has that kind of money to throw away on a piece of pie in the sky?"

"It seems that Bob does," Sandy mumbled. By the time Sylvia got home she was convinced that Sandy had blown this thing way over the top. She would wait for Bob to get home and ask him quietly and directly. Ten billion dollars, ridiculous she thought.

Bob couldn't believe what he had just heard. What kind of secret was this that Sandy Visi and Sylvia were discussing a 10 billion dollar trip to Mars over lunch at the goddamn Art Museum? Bob looked directly at Sylvia and pleaded

"please don't ever utter another word about what you heard today, believe me people have been murdered for less."

"Oh no Bob, not so fast, you can't just tell me to be quiet, you're my husband and I have the right to know when you intend to spend 10 billion dollars on something, do you even have 10 billion dollars?

"It really doesn't matter if I have the money or not, but you are not, I repeat, not going to say one more word about it", he demanded, "DO YOU UNDERSTAND."

"NO NO I don't understand", Sylvia yelled back, "all I know is that we have been married for 20 years and always treated each other with great respect and now you're talking to me like I work for you." Taken by surprise at her outburst Tosky took a deep breath, looked at his wife and said

"all right let's talk."

Chapter 4

THE JOURNEY BEGINS

The view from our observation tower was expansive on the South Dakota plains. An unmanned one eighth scale model of the DREAM vehicle was hovering 100 feet off the ground without a tether. Our remote operator in the tower cautiously manipulated a joy stick while recording the vehicles response; tilt, roll, up and down, flying the machine seemed almost trivial. The first free flight test, after months of simulation and hundreds of modifications was looking very good. The only question left was the compatibility of the control software for operating the full scale vehicle. I knew instinctively that the final adjustments would be a slow, meticulous process. Tosky's Alpha ground control team were real pro's left nothing to chance, a condition needed for success in an environment where second chances are not possible.

"Hey Bill," I asked our controller, "can we use this setup for pilot training or do we wait for the final adjustments?"

"No need to wait Tom we can start training any time. Any changes made in scale up should be insignificant for test flights, but small changes over millions of miles of space travel make a big difference; it's something we have to get right before our launch date."

"Good, let's start right now, I'll take a crack at it."

"OK Tom I'll set her down and prep you on the controls. Start thinking in 3 dimensions and small incremental movements on the joy stick, if you start to lose control just let go and the bird will stabilize and loiter, push the red gun button and she'll land at home base automatically." Pretty neat I thought, all the controls were locked into GPS with a safe range of over 10 miles in any direction, although for test purposes we were restricted to 1 mile.

"Here I go" I anxiously mumbled, "my first flight." Moving the joy stick forward the dream machine instantly shot up about 100 feet.

"Easy Tom" Bill snapped like an expecting father, I instinctively let go and to my amazement the bird just stopped and hovered in the air still as a picture. "Try it again Tom, only slower, smaller movements," now just using my fingers on the joy stick I gently lowered the craft, rolled left and slowly climbed to 200 feet. As my confidence grew it seemed surrealistic, I felt I was flying myself, free as a bird and could go anywhere and do anything. Quickly gaining a feel for the sensitivity of the controls I swooped down near home base then shot straight up and silently hovered 50 feet from our control tower; moving side-ways left then right the vehicle danced at my command, like a symphony of motion and I was the conductor. An hour later driving back to my apartment outside of Pine Ridge, a contentment came over me, a relaxed feeling of accomplishment, we were really on our way I thought.

The Sioux Indian reservation in South Dakota, a sparsely populated 5,500 square mile expanse, gave us the unimpeded opportunity to develop the DREAM machine outside the prying eyes of Government and Aerospace bureaucrats. Early in my career I had teamed with tribally owned companies and knew that the tribes operated under sovereign immunity, as separate countries inside the USA, with their own laws, police force and legally in control of their own boarders and the Sioux had the largest reservation in the country. After several weeks of negotiations we managed to lease a 20 square mile remote parcel on the reservation at the sum of 1 million dollars a month. Considering the privacy and lack of federal regulations it was certainly worth it. Hell we literally had our own private army; tribal law enforcement watched our backs constantly patrolling our site.

I was first introduced to the Oglala Sioux tribe thru David Red Cloud, the great grandson of Chief Red Cloud who along with 350 tribal men, woman and children were slaughtered by the US Army at Wounded Knee. David ran a school for young Indians teaching them a trade, manufacturing and installing solar heating units that were used extensively throughout the reservation. David was kind enough to set me up at his facility and I spent a week with him trying to understand what the Tribe would or could do for the project. When told of our plans David laughed out loud.

"Tom as you can see our tribe is very poor, many of our members live in small shacks, utilities are a constant problem for old folks and convincing younger Indians to remain on the reservation is a struggle. However the glue that keeps it all together is the land, that's really all we have, it's a spiritual relationship, and forgive the expression, we still don't trust white eyes and certainly not the Feds."

"Well David, at least we have one thing in common I don't trust the Fed either but it seems to me there is a profitable way to further both our goals without violating the land."

"Maybe Tom, you'll get your chance, but you'll have to convince the council and the chief and that won't be easy."

The New Plains Teepee

A presentation to the council was made and while waiting for the Tribes decision, I had the opportunity to witness first-hand the life style of the Sioux Indians on the South Dakota plains. David was right, the poverty was extensive and extreme and life was hard for most inhabitants, but there was a difference from the inner city poverty I was use to seeing back east. For one thing many of the Sioux lived on several acres of ground complete with a horse or two, a family dog and several head of buffalo that seemed to roam free and served as a cash crop; for many their only source of income. Shot and harvested on site by residents, the animals were butchered, weighed and paid for on the spot by meat producers out of Rapid City – there were no fences, property taxes or building codes and the land provided most of the nourishment for these animals. A self-sufficient Eco System, I thought, created by nature and caring inhabitants, mutually respecting each other. I was beginning to understand the spiritual connection to the land that David had mentioned and wondered how my own culture missed this connection so badly.

The Author At Wounded Knee Cemetery

The past year had been full of surprises and exacted an immense cost both in material and changes in the lives of all of us involved. The Atlas episode was still a concern and I began reminiscing how we got into that mess and how it would eventually end up. After Joe and Lana's kidnapping debacle Tony Colby was already looking for ways and means to shut down any further covert activities by Atlas; he had promised to help Joe and he meant to do it. Without any evidence law enforcement couldn't respond, besides we had taken matters into our own hands and probably violated more laws than Atlas. Pondering the question the answer came suddenly, Lana was dead! Marie got the call from Joe Campo and transferred it to my office.

"Joe its Tom what the hell happened?"

"She's dead Tom" Joe replied in a painful voice, "the hospital told me she died of smoke inhalation in an apartment fire."

"That's horrible Joe I'm sorry, what can I do, is there anything you need?" Joe shot back

"I TRUSTED YOU, YOU SAID YOU WOULD TAKE CARE OF THIS, WATCH OVER HER, I guess that was all bull shit and now she's dead."

"No! No! Joe don't think that way, you don't know…….. Joe, Joe are you there?" the phone was dead.

Jeff George was in a pensive mood when his secretary's voice came over the intercom.

"Mr. George, Jack Bickford's on line 1."

"Hello Jack good to hear from you, how are things at Atlas?"

"Listen Jeff I'm getting concerned, our plan B has been compromised, questions are being asked about my relationships with ArmorTec and your deceased assistant, apparently Joe Campo has been snooping around. I just hung up with a private eye he hired that I've known for years."

"Christ Jack, Campo was Lana's boyfriend. I tried to plug that leak several months ago."

"Yea and you messed up big time", Bickford hissed. "Just make sure you make this one go away or we'll all go down, and Jeff keep this in mind you're in this as much as me."

Hanging up, George's face was beet red – for the past 20 years he climbed the corporate ladder at Black Rock with a can do attitude, handling every lousy job and screw up that came his way. Corporate bosses trusted him and let him run his own show as long as the money kept rolling in; but this was different, Lana had compromised Black Rocks intelligence but she didn't deserve to die, and now he knew exactly what Bickford expected. He also knew this had to stop and needed to find a way out.

The EMT that transported Lana to the hospital kept looking around as he answered Joe Campo.

"Look, Mr. Campo I shouldn't be talking about this, I could lose my job." Joe smiled and replied.

"Don't worry no one will know" as he slid a hundred dollar bill into his shirt pocket. "All I'm asking is for you to tell me the details of the pick-up; did you notice anything unusual, any people near-by, anything?" The EMT paused.

"No nothing that I can think of; these things are always different, circumstances are never the same."

"Was she alive in the ambulance?"

"She had a pulse, but it flat lined before we got to the hospital."

"Didn't you try to revive her?"

"Of course I did Mr. Campo, I paddled her 3 times, after the first shock I opened her eye lids and, ...wait a minute there WAS something unusual there........."

"What, what" insisted Joe.

"Her eyes were completely dilated, that's not normal."

"What do you mean?"

"I mean her eyes were dilated, I've seen a lot of corpses and the only ones that had dilated pupils were OD's."

"What D's," Joe asked intently.

"Drug overdoses Mr. Campo."

Driving home Joe had been suspicious and now he was sure, Lana was a health freak, wouldn't take an aspirin. The bastards killed her he thought and he meant to find the evidence and hang her murder around their necks. Putting a plan together, his train of thought was broken by the ring of his cell phone...

"Hello" Joe answered.

"Mr. Campo," a familiar voice came over the line, "its Jeff George from Black Rock." Joe was stunned, his anger welled up in his throat so fast he couldn't utter a word, "Joe Campo, are you there?" George asked again.

"Yea I'm here," Joe finally replied doing all he could to control his voice, "what do you want?"

"Joe I need to talk with you tonight."

"I'm listening."

"No not over the phone, can you meet me at the Radisson on south west 10th street about 7."

"I'll be there," Joe replied and abruptly hung up. Making a U turn thru the Maryland house rest stop on 295, Joe floored his car reacting to the call, the balls of this guy he thought, I need to get my hands on him, make him confess or I'll kill him. 10 minutes later, his anger under control he realized he still needed a plan, maybe some muscle too. Reaching for his cell he called the only other guy who had a score to settle in this whole mess.

"Hello Jim, it's Joe Campo."

"Oh hi Joe, heard about Lana, I'm really sorry, just got the news today."

"Thanks Jim, any chance you still want to get to the bottom of the Black Rock problem?"

"YOU BET YOUR ASS I DO, I've been working 24/7 turning our test facility into a god damn armed camp, if they come at me again I'll be ready."

"Yea well I've got another problem, I'm not sure Lana's death was an accident, I'm meeting with Black Rock tonight and I may need a backup, can you help?" Jim was silent for a moment, thinking, Joe sounded desperate, and whatever came up he needed to be ready.

"Sure Joe, count on me, just tell me where and when."

The temporary office trailers located at our South Dakota test site were constantly filling up with excess files, samples, and extraneous electronic equipment. An additional double wide was delivered over the weekend and Phil Visi was trying to make sure it would be restricted to management personnel only. Standing outside, I found Phil at the back end and waived at him thru the window to let me in.

"Good morning Tom, sorry about the security, we really need to keep this locked down or the flight crews will turn it into a flop house." Phil was handling logistics in addition to engineering for the DREAM propulsion system and had been working 12 hour days for several weeks now.

"How's it going partner, you look like you could use a vacation, and I've got just the place, it's only 60 million miles away." Phil smiled.

"Yea and after this it'll feel like a walk in the park. Tom did you ever imagine that we would be doing this, going to Mars?"

"No, but I do know the only reason we're going are the antigravity panels. I'm still trying to get my arms around that. All of my life I've wondered what gravity really was; it never got passed a mathematical relationship between mass and distance. That never sat well with me and I never did find an answer."

"Of course you didn't lame brain," Phil interrupted, "we didn't know then and we still don't know today."

"Funny thing though," I added, "it seems we now know more about Anti-Gravity than Gravity courtesy of Dark Energy, and maybe, just maybe DREAM holds the answer I've been looking for."

"Interesting" Phil mused, "maybe your prophetic, but if we're ever going to get there we need to finalize the crew selection, lift off is only 3 months away. Each member needs to be cleared by flight and medical and tested in zero gravity, you know the vomit comet flight, it's set for the end of this month out of Rapid City."

"Yea I'm gonna love that one, where do we stand so far?"

"We have 6 primary crew members and a backup for each, counting you and I that makes 8. The entire crew will be crossed trained in flight controls, navigation, and equipment operation. That's going on as we speak. You know Colby wanted to go, he was flagged by medical,"

"He's OK with it" I said, "told him we needed someone to run the show back here, I even had a power of attorney drawn up for him while we're away. What about cargo Phil?"

"Most of its here, we're still waiting for the hybrid ground transporters, they've still got a few bugs, we'll be OK. Oh…., and wait till you hear this one, the good colonel finally got flight authorization, pulled this rabbit out of a hat……. as a result of our slow near earth speed we fall into a high altitude balloon flight category."

"A BALOON FLIGHT?", I asked in disbelief.

"You got it, Rocket power is tightly restricted but since our power source has no outward effect and no onboard fuel supply Tony convinced the FAA that we're no different than a large air lift device like a blimp; incredible, I love that guy."

"It's a brave new world Phil; before we're done they'll have to rewrite the whole damn flight book."

The flight plan was an elegant piece of celestial navigation and engineering, comfortably transporting human beings at extremely high speeds in a zero gravity environment. The trip would occur in 5 stages; near earth space; acceleration stage; deceleration stage, near mars space and touchdown. As a result of the unlimited power afforded by DREAM a constant power flight was planned, eliminating the need for extended intercept glide paths. Computing a Mars intercept point in space based on our launch date and travel time, the flight path becomes a straight line, simplifying navigation along with reduced mission distances.

The near earth stage begins at lift off, traveling upwards at a predetermined angle and at a constant speed of 50 MPH. The slow speed complying with FAA guidelines also minimizes the lifting stress on interconnecting ship components. A silent, all weather lift off transports the crew to an altitude of 50 miles one hour later. After confirmation from ground control and a final systems check a go for high speed space flight is issued allowing the power panels to reconfigure for the next stage.

The acceleration stage propels the ship over 50 million miles, approximately 70% of the journey. The power panels, now deployed at 60 degrees, provides a constant acceleration at $\frac{1}{2}$ G or 16 ft/Sec squared and a comfortable gravity induced environment for the crew. At this acceleration rate the speed of the ship reaches 300,000 MPH after one full day and continually accelerates for the next 3 days exceeding a speed of 1 million MPH. Inside the ship the constant smooth acceleration is not perceptible and the crew is unaffected by the extreme speeds, simply feeling a lighter than normal gravitational type pull.

The third, deceleration stage, reconfigures the power panels flipping the ship 180 degrees from its direction of flight in an aft first attitude and begins the deceleration process by applying power in an opposing direction. Again a gravity induced environment is artificially created for the comfort and safety of the crew for the balance of the journey; Power panels now deployed at 70 degrees provides the deceleration necessary for the next 2 days to intersect the Martian atmosphere at a calm 12000 MPH.

Entering the near Mars space, (the fourth stage), further deceleration is achieved, reducing velocities to 1000 MPH at an altitude of 10,000 feet. Given the lower density of the Martian air, its 1/3rd gravitational force that of Earth, and lack of FAA regulations, freedom and speed of movement within the Martian atmosphere is completely unrestrained. In addition to the primary landing site, contingency sites are available to account for changing conditions or mission requirements; hovering at altitude, multiple topographical, mineral and atmospheric scans are conducted in addition to enhanced visual observations, prior to final site commitment.

The fifth and final landing stage quickly decelerates the ship to an altitude of 500 feet over the designated landing site, and hovers for a final close surface check, before deploying adjustable foot pods in preparation for touchdown. Zeroing in on the site at a vertical descent speed of 10 feet per second, the ship comes to a full stop 10 feet above the landing site. Now in manual flight control, the pilot inches the ship down until each of the four foot pads are fully deployed and locked to maintain a level orientation. The bird has landed – Welcome to Mars.

The flight plan, briefly presented here, represents thousands of man-hours of engineering, software development, manufacturing and countless numbers of smaller details each meticulously created, categorized, stored and inspected for a single purpose. The outflow of cash was dizzying even in the early stages of the program and as vehicle construction progressed the rate of expenditures accelerated even further. Two ships were in progress, the primary mission craft, Horizon 1 and a recovery ship, Lazarus, absent the

Cargo module. Lazarus was planned as both a backup and rescue ship while Horizon 1 was in transit, but eventually would enter a planned fleet and fully fitted out for future missions. Each of the 3 sections of the craft were separately subcontracted out and designed to be stacked and quickly assembled directly on a launch pad with our Alpha team performing the final integration right on site.

The assembly operation was unprecedented, especially on such a scale but as a result of the designs rigidity and ruggedness the plan worked efficiently eliminating many intermediate processing steps provided the modules were perfectly constructed. To do so required the best in class manufacturers from around the world, most of which were nowhere near our launch site. The transportation problem was anticipated; Guppy aircraft (converted military star-lifters with large front loading holds) were readily available capable of flying globally. The Rapid City international airport had the runways to handle these planes and the surrounding South Dakota highways leading to the Sioux reservation were well paved and generally not congested; a late night or early morning delivery of double wide trailer loads would not have a traffic issue.

Progress was now moving at a frantic pace; our DREAM and Alpha teams had finally started to gel, anticipating the next step, potential problems and timely solutions. The program began to have a life of its own and with things going so well I began to look over my shoulder, wondering how long this would last; as it turned out not long! The phone call from Marie back at ArmorTec was confusing. Joe Campo and Jim Dougherty were now in hiding after a confrontation broke out at a meeting with Black Rock in DC no less. After trying to call Joe directly I hoped on a red eye to Philly that night and arrived next morning at my office. Walking in Marie looked distraught.

"I'm so glad you're here," she sobbed and with that ran into my arms shaking.

"Easy, easy," I whispered holding her, "whatever it is we'll take care of it." A short while later sitting in my office Marie collected her-self and relayed the contents of Joe Campo's telephone conversation.

"Tom I heard yelling in the background as Joe was talking and then what sounded like gun fire."

"Gun fire?" I asked becoming alarmed, "is Joe OK?"

"I think so, everyone was yelling so much all I heard after that was Joe hollering JIM get the car, GO, GO, GO and the phone went dead."

The knock on my condo door interrupted dinner and persisted as I walked down the hall hollering.

"Keep your shirt on I'm coming," opening the door Joe Campo and Jim Dougherty scrambled in like a couple of scared rats.

"Tom glad we found you home," Joe stammered in an excited voice, "did Marie get a hold of you?"

"Thank God you're OK, yes she did…. you want to tell me what the hell is going on." Joe and Jim had a drink and settled in.

"I lost my temper," Joe went on and explained Lana's not so accidental death and Jeff George's telephone call; "we met George in the lobby of the Radisson night before last, he told me Lana was set up to look like an accidental death and that he had nothing to do with it. An exec at Atlas by the name of Jack Bickford ordered it after he found out that Lana compromised Black Rock's intelligence and identified him."

Describing the conversation during the meeting Joe continued, George was remorseful.

"Joe I swear I didn't know, never expected it to go so far."

"Yea but you let it happen, and that makes you responsible; time to pay the piper George, turn yourself in or I'll do it for you."

"Thought about that too Joe, somehow Bickford will stop me and I'll wind up like Lana. I know he's been tailing me and already threatened to shut me up, there has to be another way."

"Afraid not Jeff, just do it, we'll take care of Bickford." With that we left the hotel, walking to our car I stopped and called Marie to let you know what happened. In the middle of my call 2 men got behind me trying to force me in a car with another man in the back seat, I got a look at him, it was Bickford and I knew I was in deep trouble. I shoved back hard and ran yelling;

"Jim get the car"….

"I heard Joe screaming," Jim interjected, "I started running towards him, then the bastards started shooting, luckily they were amateurs, he was only 20 feet away and they missed 3 times. I had no choice, it was us or them. I pulled out my pistol and unloaded a clip into the back seat of their car, a minute later I wheeled my car around and picked up Joe." That night the news reported that an Atlas executive was murdered in a drive by shooting.

A month had passed since the Radisson shooting and things were starting to heat up. Jim Dougherty had been implicated and was wanted for questioning. He felt the shooting was justified and so did I, but a killing occurred and proving his innocence could be problematic. After some soul searching Jim did not want to turn himself in and needed to buy some time and I agreed to help.

"Look Jim, you need to get out of DC law enforcement jurisdiction. You haven't been accused of anything and you're not breaking any laws by moving away."

"OK but where to Mr. D."

"Jim, please call me Tom, you're making me feel old." Jim frowned and hesitated, almost like he was trying to pronounce a foreign word.

"Tom… it is then."

"Better Jim, Better," I assured him, "I'm sending you to our test site in South Dakota, you'll be safe there for the time being, US law enforcement has no jurisdiction there and I'm sure you can help out."

"Right Mr.....ahh, right Tom" he stammered, "I'll catch the next flight out today, and thanks I won't forget this."

"Jim, you've been a loyal employee and Bickford deserved what he got, I would have done the same thing. You don't owe me anything."

Once on site Jim quickly integrated himself into our flight team and was making his presence felt as they closed in on our upcoming launch date. At my weekly progress meeting via remote access, Phil Visi asked;

"What the hell did you promise this guy Tom, he's like a machine, works non-stop 24/7."

"Maybe a ride," I said, "Let's see if we can fit him in."
"He's a good tech," Phil added;

"I know he has a military background and could also fill a security slot, something I've been trying to figure out without adding additional personnel, what do you think?" "I can personally vouch for that Phil, if you can get him ready in less than a month."

Chapter 5

THE 2ND BATTLE AT WOUNDED KNEE

Back in South Dakota tribal law enforcement had reported some suspicious activity and had to escort several people off the reservation for trespassing restricted areas near our site. It seemed innocent enough until I got a call from the chief.

"Tom D'Antonio, Chief Pierce here."

"Hello chief how are you, what can I do for you?"

"I'm fine Tom, wanted to let you know that I got a call from the department of the Interior, they're insisting that I allow an inspection team from the Aerospace Industry access to your site."

"For what?" I asked emphatically.

"Don't know yet, but I told the bastard no one steps foot on that site until I know what it's for and I want it in writing, they're not one of my favorite organizations. Tom this has nothing to do with your activities, it's a tribal issue" and he added in an ominous tone, "WE WON'T LET THIS HAPPEN AGAIN!"

Tribal law enforcement was now on full alert. In addition to our own security Indian patrols double checked anything that moved in or near our facility. I knew something was going on when I saw the road blocks setting up on route 13, a main highway coming in from Wounded Knee. The Indian guards were tight lipped and feelings were running high. The chief didn't answer my calls and I instinctively reached out for David Red Cloud.

"Hello David it's Tom D'Antonio."

"Hi Tom what's up?"

"I think you know David, why all the secrecy and why are you blockading roads?"

"Tom you need to stay out of this, not my words came directly from the Chief. This morning we stopped a caravan of police vehicles trying to escort a group of officials with a subpoena to your site."

"Damn David, why didn't you let me know, maybe we could help."

"Tom don't mess with 500 years of history, this is not your fight and there's no way you can help, even if you could the Tribe wouldn't accept it."

"I don't understand David." "That's because you're not listening Tom."

"I did David, heard every word you said."

"I mean with your heart not your head," he went on, "you must understand, we come from a proud warrior culture and we're prepared to give our lives for this cause. You look at this as a trespassing issue, we look at this as a desecration of our land, the life blood of our Tribe, it's now a question of honor and there's no turning back." I was silent for a long moment;

"Alright David, I'll stay out of it, but you gotta keep me informed, will you do that?"

"Sure Tom, I'll let you know if anything starts to break."

Take off in the converted 707 was uneventful, and the open padded cabin offered no amenities or seating except for an unobstructed view of the earth's horizon at 25,000 feet. The zero gravity ride, otherwise affectionately known as the vomit comet would soon live up to its moniker. Sixteen of us sat on the cabin floor 5 feet apart as the plane began its first dive generating a negative 1 G, simulating conditions in outer space.

"Woa," I yelled, as I began to float and bounce around the cabin. "This is fantastic how long does it last?"

"60 seconds on each dive," replied our instructor, "try to stabilize yourself and control your movements, you won't have the luxury of padded surfaces in a space ship."

"Yea right," hollered Phil, "I'm so dizzy the walls look like they're spinning." The instructor grabbed him by the leg.

"That's because you're spinning like a top, loosen up and fixate on one spot, otherwise you'll get disoriented and if you do make sure you grab one of those upchuck bags and don't miss." Phil and several others looked like they were ready as we pulled out of the dive. "OK gentlemen that was your first taste of zero gravity."

"More like this morning's breakfast," I mumbled.

"We'll do it again as soon as we get to altitude. Until you acclimate yourself to these conditions, don't rely on your senses use your brain to figure out your orientation and your body will adjust, Got it!" Before anyone could respond, he blurted out, "OK here we go again." This time I focused on one spot at the end of the cabin and realized my dizziness was caused by tumbling.

"Son of a bitch," I thought, this guy knows what he's talking about, my body started to stabilize and I was able to push off and fly to the spot I was staring at. Floating around now my queasiness began to subside although four others including Phil had their heads buried in the brown bags hanging on the cabin walls.

Exiting the plane all of us were a little unstable, our instructor smiled and shaking our hands said,

"Congratulations gentlemen this qualifies you as student astronauts," and added handing each of us a personalized flight certificate, "you're now part of a select group of extra -terrestrials."

"Thanks buddy" I said, "think I'll stick to my day job."

"Nothing to it Mr. D'Antonio, you'll get used to it and your body will adapt." We did this 7 times, 7 minutes in outer space I thought and most of us looked like we went thru a meat grinder, how the hell were we going to make a week in space.

The next day, the stillness of the early morning was abruptly interrupted. The distinct crack of a rifle reverberated over a bluff adjoining Wounded Knee, followed by a continuous volley of shots for what seemed like an hour. Shortly after the shooting stopped, David Red Cloud was on my cell.

"Hello Tom can you hear me?"

"Yes I'm here David, heard a lot of distant rumbling, what's going on?"

"We attempted to deliver a Cease and Desist order to escort the staties off the reservation, shouting started and a shot rang out from the caravan, then all hell broke loose."

"My God David was anybody hit?" "We had over a hundred officers not 20 feet from the caravan, what do you think happed, several men on both sides went down."

The day passed and a shaky truce was in place, but neither side relented. That night the Attorney General of South Dakota was on the phone with Chief Pierce.

"Chief, this is a bad situation, the Feds are all over us demanding that we mobilize the National Guard, we have to stop this right now before anybody else gets hurt."

"Fine Ed" the Chief replied adamantly, "just tell those clowns to pack up and get the hell off my reservation."

"Look Chief, I don't like this any more than you.....you know as well as me that Governor Grace is a State Rights advocate, but this is not the time to draw a line in the sand, we just don't need this kind of publicity and if you back off now the Fed will make it up to the Tribe." Becoming enraged at the offer, the Chief angrily ranted,

"I smell politics Ed, you can tell that coward of a Governor for me to go to hell; you know our history."

"It was a hundred and fifty years ago, for Christ sake," Ed pleaded.

"Yea well maybe you forgot about it but we didn't; I swear to you, if we all have to die here so be it, but rest assured we'll take those bastards with us."

"Damn it Chief let's be reasonable," before he could say another word Chief Pierce cut him off.

"That's my final word Ed, there's nothing else to talk about," and hung up. Chief Pierce pondered the threat and knew full well the gravity of the situation. Although the tribe maintained a sizable, well-armed force they were no match for the National Guard. His only option now would be to neutralize the caravan on site and get public opinion on their side.

David Red Cloud was the messenger, and a full court press was now on. Early the next morning David was on the phone.

"Tom I have a request from Chief Pierce,"

"Sure David, what is it?"

"Do you have any contacts with the TV networks back east?"

"Maybe, what for?" "David went on relaying the Chiefs conversation with the Attorney General last night and the response the tribe was anticipating.

"Do what you can Tom, but remember you're not a combatant."

"Got it David, I'll stay in touch." Hanging up, I thought, Public Relations was not my forte, we needed someone that had the influence and contacts to help mold public opinion and Bob Tosky was the perfect man for the job. To my surprise Tosky jumped at the chance.

"Tom glad you asked, I'm bored sitting on the sidelines here while you're having all the fun. I've been itching for a fight and I know network execs that would give their right arm for a story like this, hell their ratings will go thru the roof and maybe we can start getting free press for the Mars venture now that the cat's out of the bag."

"Easy Bob, are you sure you want to go public right now."

"Listen Tom this is my turf, trust me, if we lose we're no worse off than we are now, but if we win we'll be untouchable, it's a no brainer."

A few hours later, things began moving into high gear; a constant stream of TV crews were coming in and I was the point man. Several mobile vans were already rolling down route 13 from Rapid City asking me where the action was and where to set up. Damn, Tosky was good, I thought, waiting for David Red Cloud to answer his phone.

"Hello David, it's Tom, the TV stations are on their way, is it safe to set up behind the barricades?"

"Not yet Tom, there's been some sporadic fire down there and we've mobilized the entire reservation."

"Christ David, it sounds like you're getting ready for a war."

"More like a tactical deployment Tom, we're not planning a Little Big Horn, we're smarter than that, and we're counting on the Fed not realizing it." I couldn't help grinning at David's insight;

"So what's the plan?"

"Can't go into it now Tom, do you know the bluff that runs along the Wounded Knee cemetery?"

"Yes, sure David you took me there when I first visited the reservation."

"There's a dirt road at the east end of your property, it'll take you right to the top of the bluff, the cameras will have a bird's eye view from there and I'm pretty sure they'll be out of harm's way."

Tribal forces began to move, they first cut off the retreat route for the caravan strategically placing several bull dozers blocking the road. In the distance scores of armed Indians bunched in groups of 10 men squads formed a semicircle behind the caravan, while loud war chant music was blasted from the barricade to distract their attention. If the Staties tried to take any aggressive action they would now be caught in a deadly crossfire. Finally all activity stopped and a dead silence spread over the area like a fog, a peaceful calm before the storm.

Moments later the shrill sound of a bull horn pierced the air.

"**Drop your weapons and come out with your hands up,**" a voice from the tribe echoed, "**you are trespassing on Tribal property and you have no jurisdiction here.**" A reply came back promptly from the caravan.

"**We are here under the orders of the State of South Dakota and you are guilty of obstructing a lawful court order, clear the road and let us pass**"……..

"**We will not clear the road and if you persist you will be taken into custody by force if necessary.**" Again silence, the die was cast and orders were given to continually fire volleys over the caravan so that there could be no misunderstanding of the trap they were in.

All of the day's activity were now being broadcast around the country and would shortly be the top story on the evening news. The national debate had already begun; Tribal rights versus Federal and States rights, issues that most Americans seldom heard or knew about. National sympathy generally favored the Tribes, given their well-known history particularly Sioux history, but property rights were another story, vague and legally a labyrinth of broken treaties and promises. A clearer issue was needed to mobilize strong public opinion, an issue that could capture the imagination and interest of the public and Bob Tosky saw this immediately. Grabbing the opportunity Tosky was on the phone to his network friends at NBC and Fox selling with the zeal of a New York stock broker.

"Look Charlie, this whole thing came about because of a commercial venture that I financed. The Fed took action because my competitors cashed in political favors to put a road block in my way," Tosky went on, "it's a clear violation of contract law, play for pay, and at the highest levels."

"So what else is new, you're just telling me what you think and you don't have anything to support your allegations; by the way what the hell is this venture you're talking about?"

"A trip to Mars Charlie," Tosky casually answered.

"I'm a busy man Bob, don't have the time to waste on bullshit."

"I'm dead serious, Tosky shot back in a stern tone, "you have a TV crew right now on our launch site with a space ship standing by, check it out."

"Are you kidding me, a trip to Mars," Charlie gasped, with that Tosky described the DREAM project in detail and added,

"If you dig deeper I'm sure you'll find all kinds of corruption, congressional figures maybe even the president, your viewers would eat up a story like that, don't you think?"

"Maybe" Charlie hesitated, "yea, maybe they would."

Chief Pierce knew that time was running out before a rescue effort would be attempted by the National Guard. It was now or never and he began the bold action of his end game plan. A thousand Indian warriors started inching closer to the caravan and at the signal of a flaming arrow loosed from behind the barricade the entire force converged on the caravan. The surprised and exhausted State troopers quickly surrendered, were immediately cuffed and placed under house arrest. The aerospace execs in the caravan were outraged but too terrified to protest. After assurances about their safety they were permitted to make a statement to the press.

"I want to let our families know that we are unharmed and I have been assured by Chief Pierce that we will be free to leave the reservation shortly," came the shrill voice of the spokesman for the Aerospace reps. "We came here to conduct an environmental assessment however in view of the events of the past few days this matter will have to be settled by a court of law once we return, thank you." Turning to leave a reporter from the Fox news agency aware of the issues shouted out,

"Sir, why are Aerospace executives conducting environmental investigations for the Interior department"….. surprised by the question the spokesman hesitatingly replied,

"We have specific technical expertise for this kind of work and, and the federal government requested this service of us." Again the fox reporter shot back,

"Isn't it true that you came here to stop the scheduled launch of a new kind of spaceship for a trip to Mars not 2 miles from here?" Now becoming agitated the spokesman sternly replied,

"I told you this is about an environmental issue."

"Please answer the question sir, aren't you trying to interfere with an authorized launch of a competitor?" the reporter insisted, with that the red faced exec stammered

"That's nonsense!" and walked away.

A stream of reporters quickly invaded the launch site photographing Horizon 1 and interviewing anyone who would answer questions. That night the top story on the evening news captioned "TRIP TO MARS," "NEW ENERGY SOURCE DISCOVERED," "SECOND BATTLE AT WOUNDED KNEE" and "INVESTIGATION SOUGHT, PLAY FOR PAY SUSPECTED." Tosky was right, the cat was now out of the bag and we were untouchable. That following week the reporter population swelled, including foreign coverage, to the point where scheduled tours and briefings were conducted in groups of 10. Tosky wasted no time using his political influence and a senate investigation was quickly called for. Public opinion was running high in favor of the Sioux driven by the inflammatory journalism of the news media trying to outdo each other and the prospect of a Martian trip kept the story alive for weeks. The spectacle, a veritable Cowboy and Indian show, was beyond all expectation's, even president Hilary Clinton disavowed any responsibility and promised to personally stay abreast of the senate investigation, while reconfirming the tribes rights to Sovereign Immunity. All of this coupled with a constant onslaught of visitors, volunteers and protesters were beginning to overwhelm our resources and interfere with the program schedule. Finally by the fourth week, other national news took over the front page and we quickly resumed a catch up schedule.

Chapter 6

THE FLIGHT OF
HORIZON 1

A flight crew of 8 consisting of a captain, 1ˢᵗ officer, Physical science officer, Medical science officer, IT specialist, equipment specialist, communication specialist and a pilot were selected for the first manned Martian voyage. I assumed the role of captain but recruited a retired astronaut, John Hodges, as 1ˢᵗ officer. Phil Visi filled the Physical science slot and an MD, Susan Lee, came on board as our medical officer. Susan had spent the last 10 years of her career at NASA heading up a space science and medical staff and was recruited by Phil Visi; as Phil tells it she immediately volunteered when she learned of the trip and the people involved, felt it was a chance of a lifetime. The Geek as we call him, Jay Lanza, a computer genius would handle our IT activities. After spending 3 years in a federal penitentiary for hacking into secure government data bases, the FBI recruited him as a security asset to thwart a particularly infectious brand of cyber warfare sponsored by the Chinese Government. His work was so effective that he was completely exonerated for his past crimes and his record expunged to avoid any possible agency embarrassment if called upon in the future. He was one of Tosky's guys and we were lucky to get him. Jim Dougherty was our equipment specialist and also doubled as a security officer. Needless to say Jim couldn't wait to leave. A disk jockey and radio station manager out of Trenton NJ, Lillian Banks was our Communication specialist. I first met Lillian while doing an interview for a defense group called the Mid Atlantic Research Consortium and was immediately impressed with not only the tone and clarity of her voice but also her command and operation of the maze of audio equipment while doing the interview simultaneously. We remained friends, and on several occasions I tried to hire her only to be told "not a chance in this world." Curious enough when I approached her again for a trip out of this world, almost jokingly, she accepted. Completing the Horizon 1 crew, Hank Larson, a retired Air Force Major would pilot the ship. Hank was an F22 jockey who flew scores of combat missions over Afghanistan and Iraq. His credentials were impeccable and exhibited the composure and confidence that would be essential for the journey.

On a sunny, brisk South Dakota morning Launch day had finally arrived. At precisely 10:20AM on the 27th of September 2019, Horizon 1 would lift off. Awakened at 5:00AM for a private ceremonial breakfast the crew casually talked about the expected media coverage while speculating what the first stage of the flight would be like. After breakfast we began dressing in our flight suits, the full self-contained space suits would not be required for the flight and remained stored aboard on the ship, ready for egress on Mars or available for any emergency during the flight. Our Alpha flight control team was methodically going thru a final systems check in the observation tower, carefully flagging an extensive predetermined list of equipment functions with a go, no go, annotation viewed on a central video monitor. Anyone observing the activity wouldn't have a clue of the complexity or magnitude of the trip – it looked as though a routine equipment test was being set up; our Alpha team was that good.

Walking out of our lodging into the bright sunlight, excitement started to build as we were confronted with the roar of the spectators and inundated with questions from the media. For the first time the reality of the trip finally struck home; I had been completely preoccupied but that was all behind me now, we were really going to do this. Smiling and waving to the crowd we loaded into vans for the short trip to the launch site. On either side of the ship bleachers were set up accommodating over 500 spectators and again on exiting the van the roar of the crowd pierced our ears. I glanced at the crew to see if they were as startled as me – most looked a little lost but I sensed no regrets only excited anticipation. We entered the ship form the cargo section and climbed a gangway up into the crew quarters. Settling in we activated the on-board monitoring equipment and inspected each individual crew habitat while our pilot, 1st officer and IT specialist ascended into the command module in preparation for lift off. I could hardly contain my excitement as I sat in the captain's chair and turned on the overhead video monitor providing a panoramic view outside the ship. The rest of the crew climbed into their acceleration chairs and strapped in, the trip chronometer read 10:00AM – 20 minutes remaining and we were ready to go. Inter ship and control tower communications began to buzz, rattling off system settings and confirmations.

"T- 6:00 minutes and counting," came the voice from the control tower.

"That's affirmative" our pilot responded, "all systems are a go."

The chronometer clicked down, as our excitement reached a feverish pitch, my hands started to sweat and my stomach growled; we all looked serious except for Susan who was smiling and began to giggle.

"Don't mind me" she said, "just a nervous reaction" and continued to laugh. The count-down went on, 5, 4, 3, 2, 1 and LIFT OFF. With a light shutter the ship lurched upward and smoothly accelerated to 50 mph. Pointing a video port back at the bleachers the crowd was waving and cheering wildly, the sky above was a serene blue and all of us, mouths agape, remained tense and perfectly silent, as if we were waiting for the other shoe to drop, ending the journey and our lives in a spectacular crash. Finally Phil Visi spoke up, "I guess it worked!" at that we all laughed out-loud releasing the tension that had built up and now everyone began talking at once.

"Fantastic, just like an airliner, what's for lunch?"

"Hey I just saw a seagull."

"Hell of a lot better than the vomit comet, NASA ain't gonna believe this."

"Only the first stage" I insisted, "this is the easy part, but it's a hell of a good start." Within a half hour we reached

120,000 feet and at constant velocity gravity diminished and we began to float. Unlike the vomit comet this experience of weightlessness was exhilarating. Although strapped into our chairs the simple task of raising your arms and legs was effortless, without the stress of gravity my body completely relaxed for the first time in my life. Another half hour quickly passed and the ship came to a dead stop loitering at 50 miles altitude, while waiting for confirmation for the acceleration stage of the flight. Over the intercom John Hodges our 1st officer came on,

"Tom everything looks good, flight control gave us a go for high speed flight and they're just tweaking our heading, as soon as I get it we'll upload it to the navigation computer."

"Great John… and wait for my go ahead, I've got a few crew members here floating around like birds." Lillian Banks had insisted on trying out the zero gravity toilets and Phil had floated up to the command deck. The others including myself were simply enjoying the pleasure of unassisted flight.

All the while we were still being monitored back at mission control "OK guys fun and games are over the intercom squawked,

"Tom; we still need to get a physiological base line on all of you before high speed flight."

"OK, OK," I replied,

"Tom, please respond with an affirmative, stick to protocol."

"Got it, err, affirmative, OK people you heard the man, back in the saddle and strap in." The acceleration stage would speed the ship to over one million mph in four days while providing a comfortable half gravity induced environment.

Although the ship had an unprecedented thick skin and structural rigidity at these speeds larger micro meteors would be destructive. Early on during the development phase a plasma umbrella concept was considered to provide space born radiation protection for the crew. It turned out that energy requirements were excessive to protect the entire ship and a polyethylene liner was adopted instead minimizing exposure to an acceptable level. However it was later discovered that a plasma shield would also sufficiently disrupt any micro meteor shower to the point that the ships thick skin would provide the protection needed. Our engineers immediately seized on the idea and came up with a small nose cone plasma shield that could be powered by the ship. High speed collisions or closing speeds between micro meteors and the ship would be restricted to the forward cross section primarily at the command module. Any other collisions would occur at appreciably slower speeds and rendered harmless. The concept was impossible to physically test but extensive simulation provided an acceptable level of confidence that the design would work. This and a hundred other innovations were incorporated into the design raising concerns about the ships failure model. Although redundancy had been built into the ships critical components to avoid any catastrophic failures, all of us were well aware that prototype designs are just that, designs that are ripe for improvement and failure modes are difficult to reliably predict. In any event confidence in the ship was high and we had an expert team capable of improvising if needed.

Over the intercom came the words we were anxiously waiting to hear.

"Horizon 1 you are cleared for high speed acceleration."

"Copy that," replied our 1st officer, "captain we're ready for acceleration at your command." Glancing at our crew, and intently watching the overhead monitor,…...

"Affirmative," I replied, "mark your course, all ahead at 60% power." Without hesitation the ship started accelerating at 16 feet/second squared, the only noticeable reaction was a gentile compression of our bodies as simulated gravity immediately returned. Visually a sense of motion was not there, the expanse of space over the monitor showed no perceptible change at the speeds we were now traveling at; a condition that I fully expected to change as time went on.

An hour later the crew began walking around the deck while settling into their individual quarters. Like students moving into dorms on the first day of college, excited chatter filled the air, popping in and out of each other's quarters and taking advantage of video calling to family and friends while we were close enough to earth to have minimal time lags. I remained at the captain's station for another hour, thinking it was my responsibility to do so although I was fully aware that our 1st officer was more than capable of handling any contingency. Our flight plan called for 4 hour shifts in the command module with a minimum of 2 personnel to monitor system performance, maintenance alerts, and navigation log. 6 of us were divided into 3 rotating flight crews composed of a primary flight crew, Hodges and Larson, a secondary crew, myself and Banks, and a tertiary crew, Visi and Lee, allowing for an 8 hour interval between each crews shift. Lanza and Dougherty were designated as an emergency standby crew while available for their primary responsibilities, IT and equipment repair. In the absence of any anomaly flight crew operations were truly a redundancy; the ship literally flew itself and would not require any human interruption until stage 5, touchdown.

The sound of Phil Visi's voice broke my concentration,

"Tom, come and join us we're having our first meal, I even convinced ground control to store a bottle of Champaign on board for the occasion."

"Right you are boy" I replied jubilantly, "how's the food in this joint?"

"It ain't fine dining but at least the booze will help." As it turned out the pre-packaged food was decent, it tasted good and my only complaint was the homogeneous texture, similar to a thick yogurt. I knew it was nutritious but hoped our Alpha team had mixed in some variety. The thought of eating the same meal for a whole year was troubling. Sitting there our crew was in high spirits as if we were having lunch in a diner back home. It was unreal emphasized by the picture like live video feed of outer space on the overhead monitor and the imperceptible acceleration of the DREAM propulsion system. Looking at the chronometer I was pulled back into reality. In another hour I was due on the command deck and we were now traveling at over 100,000 mph.

Tony Colby had returned to ArmorTec, trying to keep the ship of state upright amidst all the publicity of the past few months. The US Government wanted in on the DREAM technology and weren't about to be upstaged by an independent successful journey to Mars. Tony also knew they didn't want to be associated with a possible failure and his gut told him that was the only advantage he would have.

"Tony a Mr. Alden from the Attorney General's office is on line 2," Marie buzzed in on the intercom.

"Hello Tony Colby here, how can I help you?"

"Mr. Colby, my name is Brett Alden and I'm calling on behalf of the Attorney General of the United States. We'd like to discuss your company's Martian project, and in particular the DREAM propulsion system; it's a matter of national security." Tony smiled he had expected this and innocently replied,

"Well, Mr. Alden the project has been extensively covered in the media and all the details of the trip have been carefully documented in the FAA applications, I have the case ID numbers you can have."

"Mr. Colby we're aware of the application," he insisted in an impatient voice, "we need to evaluate the design details and make sure it doesn't fall into the wrong hands. As a colonel in the US Air Force, I'm sure you can appreciate that."

"I can and do Brett, may I call you Brett?" Tony playfully asked.

"Yes, yes, Mr. Colby," Alden dryly replied, "please call me Tony,"

"Mr. Colby, ah Tony," Alden went on in a demanding voice, "you understand what I am talking about, will you or will you not provide the documentation needed?"

"Why certainly Brett but you do realize this is a proprietary project, and privately funded. What assurances can you give me that the technology won't wind up in a competitor's hands, domestic or foreign."

"You'll have the full faith and credit of the United States Government," Alden proclaimed emphatically. Tony was silent for a moment, trying not to lose his temper,

"Brett, your track record isn't that good, as they say the devil is in the details, I'm going to need specifics and then approval from ArmorTec's board before I can release any design details."

"We have the authority," Alden cut in, "under Eminent Domain we can take your designs if necessary and if you interfere you'll be guilty of a criminal offense and I assure you Mr. Colby we will prosecute." Tony's face began turning red as his anger welled up.

"Who the hell do you think you're talking to you pampas ass, before you we're out of high school, I was fighting these same battles on Capitol Hill for the past 20 years, so don't think your bull shit scares me… bring it on buster, we're ready for you!" Before Alden could reply Tony slammed the phone down. Mission accomplished he thought.

Two days on the journey had passed and all was well. Traveling at over 500,000 mph changes to the space view on the overhead monitor were now perceptible. Amazingly with this sensory impression the feeling of motion came back and we knew we were quickly going somewhere. Our intercept path had not deviated more than a half degree since lift off. Originally planned at a 28.56 degree angle from vertical we we're moving towards the sun. By the 4th day we expected to close within 83 million miles, the closest distance that our straight line intercept path would put us from the sun. The ship was performing flawlessly and yet mission control was still trying to understand the slight variation in our flight path. An anomaly, not mission critical was the response but something to keep an eye on.

By the end of the third day we had reached our maximum velocity in excess of one million miles per hour and were now ready to execute the deceleration stage. The ship would first have to stop accelerating in order to maintain our line of flight while turning, literally shutting down the power panels and then pirouette to an aft first position by slowly manipulating 2 of the power panels. The entire process referred to as DECAR (deceleration and reorient) was a tricky maneuver manually executed in order to obtain a precise heading. Our 1st officer, John Hodges, and pilot Hank Larson were at the controls.

"Hey Tom were 15 minutes away from DECAR, make sure everything that can float is locked down and everyone is strapped in their acceleration seats."

"Copy that John - OK you heard the man, let's clean the place up." After a rush of activity 10 minutes later I made a final inspection, "John were a GO for DECAR."

"That's affirmative" he replied, "3 minutes to DECAR." Watching the chronometer count down a giddy feeling came over me, was this real or a dream. Maybe I would wake up on a Star Trek movie set, step out of a stage prop and call it a day. The crew, now accustomed to the refined comfort of space travel courtesy of the DREAM propulsion system seemed completely at ease. Sue Lee and Lillian Banks were discussing ideas on space suit designs for women while Phil Visi, Jim Dougherty and Jay Lanza were touting football team prospects for the upcoming super bowl; more like a dinner party than a groundbreaking space flight. The chronometer finally counted down and the atmosphere quickly changed as the effects of weightlessness came on. Gradually the ship began to silently reorient 180 degrees to an aft first position; our only sensory impression of the maneuver was the rotation of the star view on the central video screen which had remained relatively constant up till now. A few minutes later Hodges voice came over the intercom,

"Reorientation complete captain, were right on the numbers and ready to power up for deceleration."

"Copy that, on my command…….. Commence Deceleration."

"Affirmative captain, commencing deceleration," Larson replied while redeploying the power panels to 70 degrees effecting a slightly higher G load than during the acceleration stage of the flight. Immediately we felt the weight of our bodies compress into our seats and heard the clunk of a few loosely stored personal items drop onto cabinet shelves.

"Well done gentlemen," I commented getting up from my seat, "in 48 hours we'll be making history, the first humans to land on Mars."

Later that day quickly walking out of her cubicle, Sue Lee accidentally bumped into Jim Dougherty splashing a mug of coffee over his chest,

"Careful" Jim hollered," watch where you're going."

"I'm really sorry Jim," she gasped, "let me clean that up for you," Jim held his hand up smiling,

"it's OK Sue, coffee was stale anyway."

"Just the same come on in and sit down while I get a towel to dry you off." Gently holding his arm Sue carefully dabbed at Jim's chest with a towel, "this would work better if you take your shirt off," she insisted. "Jim looked up at Sue like an obedient child and silently removed his shirt.

"Not use to this kind of care" he nervously laughed.

"I'm a doctor Jim, and before that I was an ER nurse for 4 years, so this is kind of second nature for me."

"I'm not complaining Sue, just haven't had a female touch me in a while." Sue stopped and starred into Jim's eyes,

"Me to,"

"What" Jim asked,

"Me to," Sue repeated, "I haven't been this close to a man for a while either, kind of nice don't you think?" Jim stood up and pressed his face close to hers,

"Maybe in another place, another time Sue," she leaned closer, gently touching his face and whispered

"But we're here now and who knows if there will be another time."

A transcript of Tony Colby's run in with the Attorney General's office was finally received in my email aboard ship – video conferencing was getting difficult now due to the time delays in transmission and the volume of data constantly moving back and forth between the ship and mission control. Tony was looking for confirmation and although I fully agreed with his tactics I instinctively knew he would need all the earth bound help he could get and Bob Tosky was at the top of the list. A day later things began moving fast; the Attorney General's office was determined to come to an early resolution of DREAM and had issued an Eminent Domain order. The gloves were now off and Tosky knew that despite any legal pressure he could bring to bear this would be an uphill battle. No politician would or could directly contest the issue.

"Tony, Mr. Tosky and Joe Campo are here," Marie called out over the intercom, "they're in the conference room waiting."

"Be right there, see if they want anything."

"Already done" Marie answered in a commanding tone.

"Right," Tony replied a little unsure of who was working for whom; walking into the conference room Tosky was already dissecting the Governments response.

"Good morning Tony, looks like we're between a rock and a hard place, what's your assessment of this?" Tony paused for a moment to collect his thoughts and went on,

"Eminent Domain as you know is a major obstacle and an act of last resort. Considering the potential impact of DREAM I don't think we have a valid argument to overturn the order."

"Suppose it turns out that this is politically motivated, I mean suppose one of our competitors requested or suggested this action."

"I don't think it matters Bob, it doesn't change the fact that DREAM is an important, maybe even a critical asset for any Government to possess and control; it's literally a definition of Eminent Domain." Tosky nodded,

"How about you Joe, what's your take on this."

"Not exactly my field of expertise Bob, but why fight it, why not go with it and negotiate into it what we want."

"We'll be in a very weak negotiating position," Tony responded, "the Government holds all the cards."

"Maybe not all the cards Tony," Bob added; Tony opened his arms questioningly, Tosky continued, "ArmorTec owns the technology but my company Alpha, has spent billions perfecting and applying it, that data is outside the ownership of ArmorTec and not necessarily under the auspices of Eminent Domain. It's like trying to repossess a car without having the key to start it." Joe laughed out loud,

"Nasty Bob absolutely filthy idea, I love it."

"Hey Tom, can you climb up here for a minute?" Phil Visi asked from the command deck.

"On my way Phil," I replied heading for the gangway. Climbing the spiral stairway Phil was hunched over looking intently at the Nav computer terminal. "What's up, anything wrong?"

"Nothing I can put my finger on Tom, we've had several minor adjustments to our flight path over the past hour."

"So… sounds like the Nav system is doing what it's supposed to do."

"Yea but that's more than we've had since our launch and we're an hour away from stage 4."

"What's our velocity?" I asked,

"About 36,000 mph."

"Anything from mission control?"

"Same bullshit, an anomaly, not mission critical and they're still analyzing. I don't think they have a clue at this point; we need to start investigating this ourselves, once we hit stage 4 we're committed and there's no turning back."

"Is that the only option?"

"That's the deal!" Phil was adamant.

"OK, let's get Larson and Hodges back up here and I'll get Dougherty and Lanza to start earning their pay." After quickly briefing the crew on the ships condition an action plan was immediately put into effect. If there was a malfunction everything pointed to the power panels or the navigation software. Lillian Banks stationed herself at the communication port informing mission control and providing real time metrics for the action plan. Jay Lanza started peering over the reams of navigation software code while Jim Dougherty crawled into the service bay to check out the performance of the power panels.

"Listen up everybody," I ordered, "keep the chatter down and only report anything out of spec. Make sure your communicators are set to UNIVERSAL, I want everyone to know what pops up at the same time."

After 15 minutes of silence, I questioned Banks.

"Anything from mission control Lillian?"

"Nothing yet Tom, It'll take some time for them to go through the data and then another 8 minutes just to receive any transmission."

"Copy that…. let me know as soon as it comes in." Another 5 agonizing minutes passed and the sound of our 1st officer's voice sharply pierced the silence.

"Captain the Navigation computer is automatically adjusting our flight path every few minutes now and the adjustments are growing in intensity, recommend that we switch to manual control."

"Affirmative John," I said intensely as a knot formed in the pit of my stomach. I began reminding myself that nothing, absolutely nothing works perfectly the first time; our crew had the right stuff and with any luck we'll get thru this. Shortly after our pilot reported back;

"Captain, manual control is functioning properly, still need to make constant course corrections though. We're coming up on stage 4….we should be OK I've got good control of the ship."

"Tom, recommend we commit to stage 4," Phil Visi cut in, "I think we're far safer landing than aborting and attempting a return trip in this condition. We've got the tools and it'll give us the time to figure this out and make any needed repairs." Abort, ABORT, I thought, the word hung over me like a sword ready to strike, we've come too far to stop now.

"That's affirmative Phil, "GO for stage 4."

Coming in at 12,000 mph, we were less than 250 miles from the surface of Mars. The ships power panels were now deployed at 75 degrees further reducing our velocity to maintain a constant 1000 mph descent.

"Twelve minutes to stage 5," our 1st officer's voice broke in, "will hover and loiter at 500 feet for site assessment, based on nominal readings we'll have a GO for stage 5 on your command Captain"

"That's affirmative John," no sooner had the words left my mouth the ship began wobbling from side to side.

"Hold on people," Larson yelled, "having a hard time maintaining orientation." Jim Dougherty in a loud voice interrupted,

"Power panel 3 is fluctuating badly;" before I could reply Jim was already in action "switching to manual hydraulic pump control," he added, "will try to maintain panel attitude for a direct descent."

"Stay with it Jim," I hollered in a frantic voice and shouted, "FLIGHT CONTROL, go for touch down immediately." All of Hank Larson's training would now be needed. This was familiar territory for him having landed several badly damaged Hornets on carrier decks, he was chosen just for this moment.

"That's affirmative captain," he coolly replied, "GO for touch down." The ship started to stabilize and our descent began to accelerate, "coming up on 20,000 feet," Hodges reported, "when Lillian Banks interrupted,

"Tom, mission control is asking if we want to abort, said the decision is yours."

"Too late Lillian, tell them they're 15 minutes late we're already committed and make sure they're getting flight telemetry in case we lose it."

"I've got a hydraulic leak down here," Dougherty called out in a strained voice, "don't think I can hold it much longer."

"Hurry Hank," I urged, "if we lose that panel we'll nose dive."

"Just another couple of minute's captain," he calmly replied. Aware that if Jim said he didn't think he could hold it meant complete panel collapse was imminent.

"Don't think we have a couple of minutes Hank," I resolutely replied... now that my fate was inevitable, a sense of serenity came over me, and my only thought was hell of a waste of a good ship and crew. Hank Larson had the same feeling but was thinking of a different outcome. Pushing the throttle forward the ship lurched and quickly accelerated down, he intended to make what pilots referred to as a Kamikaze landing, a high speed full power touchdown. The trick was to apply the brakes or full reverse throttle as close to ground zero as possible. Any miscalculation or panel failure and it was over.

"2000 feet captain," Hodges yelled out, "brace yourselves!" at the same time Larson hollered

"Here we go full throttle," yanking the joy stick back. Descending at over 500 mph the ship violently slowed sending a crushing G load thru our bodies. Moments later Jim screamed out

"PANEL BLOW OUT, PANEL BLOW OUT as the ship hit the ground at a bone jarring 50 mph. Luckily the cargo section foot pads were altitude sensitive and automatically deployed, cushioning the impact before rupturing the hydraulic cylinders and collapsing. The ship now listed at a 7 degree angle from vertical, close to our original planned landing site. Sitting there in a daze it took several seconds to realize we made it. I guess the entire crew had the same reaction as they all started to clap and cheer. Steadying myself while standing up I couldn't contain my relief shakily yelling,

"*Great Job, Great Job everybody, the bird has landed*............... ....Mission Control, Horizon 1 is secure, signing off"

Chapter 7
A NEW BEGINNING

Good news travels fast prompting an immediate visit from the Attorney General's office, scheduled for the afternoon. News of the Martian landing was flashed around the world and the first images of the landing sight were starting to come thru.

"How do you want to handle this Bob?" Colby asked,

"You're the point man Tony and the only person on earth that has the authority to speak for ArmorTec. Keep in mind that the details of the rough landing and ship damage haven't been released yet so there's no reason to volunteer that information, but you can't lie. If you get boxed into a corner I'll run interference for you."

"Bob I know that better than you do," Tony replied in an annoyed tone, "I meant the Eminent Domain order, what the hell do you think they're coming here for… a social visit, are we just going to turn over our technical data or demand confidentiality?"

"You're the expert," Tosky angrily shot back sensing the sarcasm, "what the hell do you think we should do."

Colby was red faced now and about to engage in schoolyard rhetoric when Joe interrupted,

"Gentlemen, GENTLEMEN, this isn't going to get us anywhere, let's calm down and get our act together." Tony was embarrassed at his reaction.

"Joe's right, I'm sorry Bob, just been on edge getting ready for a fight."

"Doesn't matter, save it for the AG's meeting…. as I was saying the operative word is accommodation," Tosky went on, "be agreeable at first until we find out exactly what they want. If my suspicions are right they probably won't know what to ask for."

"And then," Tony interrupted, "we'll only tell them what we want them to know"

"Now you've got it," Tosky replied, "first rule of hardball negotiations, He who jumps first usually loses."

Shortly after landing the crew assembled in the conference area to plan damage assessment and report back to mission control. All members except Jim Dougherty were present.

"Anyone seen Jim?" I asked,

"I haven't seen him since we landed," Sue Lee replied nervously. For a moment we all stared at each other,

"The service bay," I said jumping up, "that's where he was when we landed." Rushing over to the bay I cautiously peered into the narrow, dark gangway leading to the power panels, "Jim, Jim," I hollered, "are you in there?" A low moan was the ominous reply.

"Out of my way," Sue demanded as she scurried thru the opening frantically searching until finding a half conscious body. "Jim honey, are you all right," she asked, carefully holding his head, Jim opened his eyes and smiled,

"glad you're OK sweetheart, is the ship out of danger?"

"Every things fine darling, I'm here now, does anything hurt?"

"Can't feel a thing Sue, only problem is I can't move my legs." After removing him from the service bay on a low boy gurney the portable medical station was retrieved from the cargo hold and set up in the crew quarters. The station was state of the art including operating facilities and a full complement of medications, blood serums and a fully operable Davinci surgery unit. In Jim's case all of it would be needed to save his life and Sue Lee was determined to do just that.

In the ensuing days it was determined that the ship sustained minimal damage. The foot pads on the cargo section were a complete lose; however the crew managed to perfectly level the ship in a vertical position with the use of hydraulic jacks. The immediate concern was life support and the power panels. The crew was split into 2 groups; team A and B – Team A composed of Hodges, Larson and myself were tasked with drilling and generator operations providing the necessary water, oxygen and hydrogen components sustaining life support and power for the heavy equipment and ship operations. Team B consisting of Visi, Lanza and Banks focused on the power panels, navigation systems and communications while Sue Lee was fully occupied taking care of Jim Dougherty. Amidst all of this activity little time was available to explore the Martian expanse that we all now called home.

Mission control was fully informed now and began planning a rescue mission. Lazarus, our rescue ship was nearing completion but the suspected latent defect in DREAM had to be resolved before attempting another launch. Time, for a change was on our side; we had sufficient provisions for a whole year and possibly crashing another ship on Mars was not an option. Getting use to the 8 minute transmission lag, video communications were becoming easier, although taking up a lot of time. We quickly learned to completely say everything we needed at each iteration in order to have a coherent conversation. Normal speaking interactions were impossibly frustrating. At the end of each day Lillian Banks usually left pending communication messages for each crew member. Bob Tosky and Tony Colby were scheduled for a 6 PM video call, that's 6 PM Martian time and 10 AM Eastern Standard Time. Sitting in front of my monitor the scheduled call started downloading.

Watching Bob Tosky and Tony Colby sitting in my office was surreal,

"Good afternoon Tom," Tosky began, "Congrats on reaching Mars, I heard about the landing, just remember any landing you can walk away from is a good one. We're calling to update you on the Eminent Domain issue;" going on, Tosky described the strategy that he and Tony came up with and the results they expected. When he was finished Tony Colby continued.

"Hey you old bastard, just like you taking all the glory and leaving us with the short end of the stick and that good landing stuff is bullshit," he said laughing. "When you get back here I'm having your license revoked, so take care of yourself buddy." It cheered me up to hear from old friends and I briefly felt homesick– but Mars had a hold on me, exciting and dangerous, I couldn't let go, at least not yet. My turn on the call I agreed to the plan and signing off, expressed my total confidence in their decisions whatever the outcome.

After disassembling failed power panel #3, each component was meticulously inspected and tested – everything appeared normal and fully functional. Attention now focused on software, a much more difficult problem to uncover but much easier to repair assuming it would ever be found. Visi took it optimistically. With the panels eliminated, he considered half the problem solved and Lanza was a computer code genius. He began using his hacking days experience – how to introduce a hidden virus while eluding rigorous testing protocols and the prying eyes of so called experts. A time bomb, he suspected - a sophisticated virus residing and asleep somewhere in the operating system until activated by a unique algorithm near the end of the journey. A team, on the other hand was quickly progressing with evident results. The nuclear generator was now functioning supplying electrical power to the ship and the drilling rig. The first 100 feet of boring into the loamy Martian surface went smoothly until hitting an unsuspected solid rock layer. Luckily the rock formation only extended some 50 feet and after breaking and replacing several sections of extension rods, drilling resumed unimpeded.

Working in the Martian environment was challenging; each morning, after chowing down our red pre-packaged breakfasts, planning the day's activities, getting into our exterior space suites and replenishing life support initially occupied most of the early AM hours. 8 hour shifts were planned divided into 2 four hour sessions to accommodate our white, pre-packaged lunch and break time to discuss any problems that came up. Work activity generally stopped at 6 PM when temperatures started to plummet from a balmy 100 degrees F during the day to a frigid negative 90 degrees F as daylight faded. Along with the rapid temperature drop, thermal winds clocked as high as 160 mph usually swept over our landing zone. The 2 redeeming features of the Martian environment, it's extremely thin atmosphere and 1/3rd Gravitational load that of Earth made high wind pressures feel like a 15 mph breeze and allowed us to effortlessly move about in our 75 pound space suites, lifting and moving materials and equipment like a horse. In any event by the end of the day a physical weariness was there and the mundane blue pre-packaged dinners began to look like fine dining.

At 250 feet into the ice pack drilling operations were stopped.

"Tom that's more than enough to supply our water needs for the next century," John Hodges said,

"OK lets swap out the drill bit and extension rods," I replied, "Hank and I will start stacking the heating coils and thermal flow pipe while you back out the drill."

"Copy that," John nodded and added, "sure you want to leave this stuff laying around loose, it's close to quitting time."

"What the hell are you worried about, Martian vandals? If these pipes are missing tomorrow I'm walking off this job and going back to Jersey." We reached the top of the ice pack at 800 feet, estimated to be 2000 feet thick; at 250 feet into the pay we could harvest as much as 850 billion gallons of untainted H2O limited only by the ability to thaw and pump it to the well head. Not bad I thought, aside from the price of a one way trip, you couldn't beat the cost of our utility bill. Once the heating coils and flow piping were installed pressure tanks stored in the cargo bay would be moved close to the well head for oxygen and hydrogen storage and dispensing. Supplied by electrolysis operations powered by the nuclear generator, the oxygen tank is further piped to the ship creating a permanent habitable environment and the hydrogen tank, now a veritable gas station would refuel the vehicles and equipment brought on this and any future missions. Although we still had over 3 months of oxygen stored aboard Horizon 1, I wouldn't rest until the installation was complete and operating.

Sue Lee had stabilized Jim Dougherty and for the past week was conferring with medical staff back at mission control on anticipated procedures and medical protocols. Jim had broken his back in the landing. Unsupported and in an awkward position the crash landing completely compressed and ruptured his L3 and L4 Lumbar Discs and laterally precariously fractured his spinal column. Sue knew that any unsupported movement would be instantly fatal and methodically manipulated his lower body for necessary bodily activities. Complicated back surgery was out of the question, but minor procedures could be performed with the help of the Davinci unit and recuperation over time was a real consideration under the present circumstances. In the meantime B-Team at Sue's insistence began setting up permanent crew quarters in the cargo section anticipating de-coupling the rest of the ship from the cargo bay as soon as the power panel problem was corrected.

"Hey buddy, how you doing?" Phil Visi asked standing next to Jim's bed.

"A lot better Phil, I'm even starting to get feeling back in my legs."

"That's great Jim, you'll be up and around in no time and that's no bullshit, got that directly from Sue. We moved the vehicles out of the cargo bay yesterday and after life support is permanently hooked up were going to relocate the medical unit and your quarters down there."

"Sounds good Phil but why go thru the trouble now?"

"Just part of the process Jim, we're shooting for de-coupling as soon as Lanza resets the Nav software, don't want you crashing a second time."

Chief Pierce and David Red Cloud arrived at the launch pad facility as scheduled. Several members of the Alpha team were waiting to escort them into the conference area to meet with Alpha's President and flight director.

"Good morning Chief, Hi David," Al Jacobs said standing up and shaking hands, "this is Harold Perot our President gentlemen."

"A pleasure to meet you Chief and David," Perot cordially smiled,

"Same here Mr. Perot," Chief Pierce replied.

"Please call me Harry," Perot insisted, "now how can I help you chief?"

"We need to talk with Tom D'Antonio Harry, it's a tribal matter that Tom was involved in."

"I'm sure we can arrange that for you Chief, Al can handle the details, but as you know Tom is 80 million miles away and we're here, I've been a lifelong student of Sioux history and it would be my pleasure to help in any way." "Interesting," Chief Pierce replied in a monotone,

"And why is that?"

"I was raised by an aunt who was a third generation Cherokee and from my earliest years she read Indian lore to me each night at bedtime....I guess it stuck and after she passed I continued to follow the progress of the major tribes including the Sioux." Surprised at the assertion Chief Pierce changed his tone,

"Well maybe you can help Harry; it's just that we prefer to have Indians solve Indian problems...Tom was an exception."

"If it makes any difference my genealogy isn't clear but there's definitely Indian ancestry in my blood lines." Chief Pierce was silent for a moment then looked up and nodded at David Red Cloud. David began describing in detail the issue that was before the Tribe...The Department of Indian Affairs notified the Tribe that they would not be eligible for Grant funding as long as the tribe maintained a for-profit commercial space flight facility on the reservation; Chief Pierce added,

"After what happened at Wounded Knee they wouldn't dare shut you down by trespassing again, this time it appears they're trying to get us to do it for them."

"I see," Harry said in a serious tone, "Chief give me a few days to discretely look into this; I'll get back to you in a week." Standing up to leave, the chief handed Perot a letter.

"One more thing Harry, can you send this message to Tom and the crew of Horizon 1?"

It was Sunday and the constant workload over the past few weeks was telling – we all needed a break. Since touch down the crew had stayed within the limited perimeter of our landing zone and today, I thought, it's time for a day off and maybe a change of scenery. The hybrid transport vehicles we're stationed alongside the Cargo bay, fueled and ready to go. I wanted to try a short run at first, maybe a mile or two – close enough to walk back in the event of a breakdown. Phil Visi and I we're suited up and ready to go about noon, while the rest of the crew slept in and attended to personal matters.

"I'll drive Phil," I said getting into the vehicle, "you're riding shotgun today."

"Good, I'll just sit back and catch some Martian rays, any idea where you're going?"

"Thataway" I said, pointing and hitting the throttle. The vehicle immediately jumped forward speeding out into the open Martian terrain.

"Easy, EASY Tom," Phil hollered, hanging on, "we've only got 2 of these things."

"YAHOO," I yelled, easing off the accelerator, "damn engine has a hell of a lot of torque on the low end, how fast can she go."

"I'm afraid to tell you," Phil nervously replied, "let's just say it'll cruise at 40 mph on a flat surface." Traveling at 25 mph we quickly left our LZ in the distance and headed out to a steep bluff. The reddish Martian soil resembled clay, but other than the top surface sand, about an inch thick the subsoil was firm and provided good traction. Reaching the bluff, I looked at Phil questioningly,

"We can climb a 10 degree grade, but take it easy or you'll spin your wheels." Driving slowly up the bluff the vehicle easily handled surface bumps and came to a stop at the crest, about 500 feet above the surface below. Climbing out of the vehicle, a stunning panoramic vista presented itself, providing an unobstructed view of the Martian landscape for miles in any direction. Mountainous areas, mesa's and valleys stretched out before us, changing colors from red to tan and shades of grey and back to red again. Even though the Landscape was barren, showing nothing green or growing, nevertheless the view was breathtaking, having a unique kind of natural beauty. Standing there in awe, we both wondered if this would be the next home for future generations.

Martian Landscape

An hour later, after describing our adventure for the rest of the crew, Lillian announced that we had received a message from the Sioux Nation with instructions to broadcast it to the entire crew. The message, now downloaded to the central video monitor read;

> "To the Crew of Horizon 1 – You have bravely journeyed beyond the bounds of Earth to another world where no man has ever gone. Know that the entire Sioux Nation is of one spirit with you. You began this Journey from our reservation and have landed on another. Remember to honor and respect the land - No matter the world the land will always provide for you and keep you safe."

On Behalf of - Chief Pierce and the Lakota Sioux People

Two large Government vans pulled into ArmorTec's parking lot with 5 men in each vehicle. Peering out of her window Marie quickly buzzed Tony Colby on the intercom,

"Tony the AG and company are here…I think we're going to need a larger conference room."

"Show them in Marie, and remember we're being polite today." Bob Tosky sitting with Tony laughed.

"Let them wait awhile; I'll bet you half of them don't know why they're here."

"You're right Bob," Joe Campo added, "I use to serve as a consulting accountant for GAO… usually contacted the last minute and told to show up and look serious never knowing what the hell the issues were." Five minutes later, Tony led the way into the conference room, and after making introductions an uncomfortable silence filled the air.

"Colonel Colby I believe you know why we're here," Brett Alden, the AG's point man said.

"I do Brett, how do you want to proceed?"

"Were obligated to advise you of your rights and responsibilities under the Eminent Domain order gentlemen," Alden answered, and proceeded for the next 15 minutes to read a mind numbing rendition of the order in its entirety. "Do you understand the order?" Alden asked when he finished;

"I think so Brett," Tony replied.

"Well Colonel, If there are no questions I'd like to start collecting the technical data, my staff is here to help your employees meet compliance standards."

"Brett I don't think that's necessary. You're welcome to make copies of any of the DREAM files that we have."

"Yes thank you Colonel," Alden replied impatiently, "but it's essential that we receive the data in a coherent way and interview your design principles." Tony shook his head looking at Tosky as he interrupted,

"I'm afraid that's impossible Mr. Alden, you see the people you're looking for aren't here and may be away for quite a while."

"Mr. Tosky I have orders from the highest authority in the US Government," Alden asserted, "and I have at my disposal unlimited funds and manpower to find and retrieve anyone involved in this project, anywhere on the globe."

"You'd have to go a little bit further Brett," Tosky replied, "we're not trying to be obstructive but the personnel you want are on Mars right now"........Alden caught off guard paused for a moment with an agitated look,

"We can wait, when do you expect them back?"

"I guess you haven't heard Brett," Colby cut in, "the ship crashed landed on Mars, and we don't know when or if they'll ever get back." Alden slumped back in his chair with a blank look on his face.

"Didn't know that," he mumbled passively," I'll have to get back to you after I pass this information along Colonel."

"You do that Brett," Tony replied, "we'll be here."

Bob Tosky frowned as he paced the conference room floor,

"I thought that went well Bob," Joe said smiling, "looked like Alden was about to have a stroke when Tony told him about the crash."

"Yea well I'm not so sure… they may be smarter than they look."

"What do you mean?" Tony asked.

"For one thing they do understand that the technical data owned by ArmorTec is not enough, didn't expect that, and I was told that the Department of Indian affairs is trying to shut down our launch site."

"When did that happen?" Tony asked in a surprised tone, "and why the hell didn't you say something?"

"Take it easy, only heard about it this morning and I'm still trying to get the details."

"Look Bob we're not a couple of flunkies hanging around here," Joe interrupted in an agitated voice,

"I've been kidnapped, shot at and got a girlfriend murdered for Christ sake, so don't tell me to take it easy, if we're not going to work as a team tell me now and I'll walk." Tosky, surprised at the outburst, stared at Joe for a moment. Catching his breath, he said calmly,

"I know that Joe; should've said something but I didn't want to chance that coming out at the meeting until we know how to handle it." The room was awkwardly silent for a while before Tosky went on, "since we are a team and I'll keep that in mind, you should also know that several major players in the transportation industry have offered to buy DREAM licenses."

"Before that goes any further Tom needs to know about that," Tony responded."

"You heard Tom as well as me Tony," Tosky adamantly replied, "it's our decision at least until he returns; in any event it's a long process and we're only at the talking stage. What I'm concerned about now is security…. just a feeling though, old habit, the Government seems to know more than they should."

Since the crash landing the Alpha team had been meticulously peering over flight telemetry. When questioned by Tony nothing significant was found - so far only a few minor anomalies. A minor anomaly, Tony mused, that's probably what king Priam thought when he saw the Trojan horse. Maybe Tosky was right, time to look inside ArmorTec.

"Marie," Tony buzzed on the intercom, "can you get me a list of employees that have been here for at least a year?"

"Sure Tony, what are you looking for?"

"I'm not sure, want to get to know each of them, their profiles, work histories, education, relatives, **everything** - we may have a security leak."

"I'll be right in," Marie replied, "maybe I can help."

38 employee folders were neatly spread out on the conference room table as Tony began glancing at their names.

"The first thing we need to do is prioritize our efforts,"

"explain that to me?" Marie replied.

"OK, which employees do we know the least about of the most recent hired?"

"That's easy," Marie answered and quickly pulled 4 files off the table. "We have 2 engineers, a draftsman and a secretary." Tony began to methodically review their resumes looking for any oddity or possible link to competitors or Government agencies. All of them looked normal not even a minor anomaly Tony smiled – the engineers were new grads with limited work experience and the secretary was really an intern file clerk still in school. The draftsman was experienced and had a solid work history, primarily in the electronics industry but nothing unusual or evidence of any discernible link. Over the next 4 hours the rest of the employees were given a once over setting aside only 2 additional names.

"Alright I came up zippo, not a clue, let's go to the next step."

"And that is?" Marie asked.

"We have 3 possible candidates - the 2 additional process engineers and the draftsman, start calling their former employers." Marie looked confused,

"what do I ask them?"

"Just get a conversation going, tell them we need a recommendation for a possible promotion."

Arriving at ArmorTec the next day Tony was surprised to find Joe Campo talking with Marie.

"Morning Joe, what the hell are you doing here so early?"

"Thought you could use some help, check your email yet?" … Before Tony could answer Joe went on, "we got an update from Alpha last night, Jay Lanza found a bug in the ships Nav computer software and not just a bug - they called it a malicious virus, in other words we were sabotaged."

"Son of a bitch," Tony hollered "how the hell could that happen with all the protocols and testing that we went thru?"

"Don't know Tony," Joe replied, "but it happened and that's exactly what we need to find out before a rescue mission can be launched." Tony's suspicions were now off the charts and he and Marie began pressing prior employers;

"don't just sit there Joe," Tony ordered, "pick up a phone and start digging."

"Nah, not my bag - got a better idea, if you want to catch a thief follow the money trail, let me see what I can find out." By the end of the day nothing had turned up and frustration was setting in.

"Dammit," Tony said throwing his hands up, "nothing, absolutely nothing, how about you Joe?"

"I've tracked down the accounts but I'll need to make a visit tomorrow to get deposits, takes a personal touch."

"Everything I've heard was polite chatter," Marie added, "great guys, works well with staff, even had a co-worker tell me he was sorry one of them left, could of used him on a hot programming job."

"Programming job," Tony yawned, "who was that?" "Rummaging through her notes," Marie looked up in surprise.

"It's Mark Hally."

"Mark the draftsman?" Tony asked sitting up, Marie nodded, why the hell is a draftsman doing programming work, he wondered; "now that's what I call an anomaly…. I think it's time to call in a pro."

Jay Lanza couldn't contain himself as he excitedly described the virus discovered in the Nav software.

"It's really a thing of beauty, my gut told me it was a time bomb and that's exactly what it turned out to be."

"I thought the software was scrutinized down to the last byte Jay," I asked, "how the hell did it slip by?"

"Had me stumped to, unlike most viruses which actively reside somewhere in the operating system, this one was totally invisible and asleep just waiting for a wake up signal."

"You're telling us that out of all the data, terra bytes for Christ sake, flowing thru the Nav computer, this virus could distinguish a unique signal even though it was dead?" Phil skeptically asserted, "can't be done."

"Give that man a CIGAR," Jay proclaimed, "that's exactly what the bastard wanted it to look like; you see in this case the virus was disguised as an inactive clock along with millions of other functional clocks in the software, so at best, in the unlikely event that a programmer would query it's function it only shows up as a nominal file or an extraneous, insignificant piece of data, this guy was really good."

"Yea well this good guy almost got us killed," I said, "and if it was so invisible how the hell did you find it hidden in all that data so fast?"

"Simple, he's good, very good but I'm better,"

"And that's it, that's your answer," Phil interrupted?

"No there's more," Jay continued, "he used what we call a dead man's clock, a tricky algorithm preprogrammed to receive a unique universal signal, a precise time down to a millisecond from the ships chronometer, a time occurring just before touchdown, then waking and blowing up the power panel controls. I suspected as much and only had to look thru the stage 5 data just before touchdown, SOOO, not terra bytes but a few thousand lines of programming."

Listening to Jay's boasting I burst out laughing,

"Not bad Jay, not bad, so I assume you've gotten the bug out and reprogrammed the Nav computer."

"Not finished yet Tom; Larson, Hodges and I are getting ready to test the software and simulate a return flight. We should be ready in a day or two."

"Good, good, just make sure we get it right, we still need to detach from cargo, schedule that as soon as possible. That's our home now and I want to button it down and make sure it's fully operational before we leave."

Ever since his meeting with Chief Pierce, Harry Perot was determined to get to the bottom of the Governments threat to cut funding for the Sioux. He held a familiarity and admiration with Indian culture since childhood and this new Government reprisal began to take on an unexpected personal dimension. Prior to joining Alpha, Harry was appointed by President George H.W. Bush as Deputy Secretary of Homeland Security in charge of the directorate's partnership with local government's domestic intelligence sharing network. He instinctively knew that somewhere in that network's maze of communications he would find the real purpose and authors of the reprisal. Although out of the agency for over 6 years now, Harry still maintained close relationships with senior Federal managers and State staffers. A few phone calls later a faxed authorization from the Department of Indian Affairs was on his desk detailing grant funding exclusions for the Sioux reservation.

"Hello Jeremy, its Harry, thanks for the info."

"No problem Harry, glad to be of service, do you need anything else?"

"Looks official enough, but you know as well as me DIA must have had their bureaucratic arm twisted half off to send a document like this."

"Yea I thought so too Harry, completely out of character…. so what?"

"I wonder who's pulling the strings," Harry casually asked. The South Dakota homeland security chief was silent for a few seconds.

"Where you going with this Harry? Anything more could be construed a security breach."

"Sure Jeremy sure, I would never ask you to violate your trust, I'm just trying to do some advocacy work for the Tribe - all I need is a solid lead." Jeremy laughed,

"So now you're a lobbyist, a beltway bandit."

"No not really," Harry quickly responded, "I still have living Indian relatives, its personal, and I'd like to try to right a wrong."

"I didn't know that Harry, sorry"….. Jeremy continued, "I'm only speculating now but If I were you I'd look in DoD specifically missile command, I hear they have very cozy relations with several large-influential Aerospace companies,"

"which ones?" Harry pressed.

"Now that's enough," Jeremy adamantly replied, "that's as far as I go."

24 hours after Tony Colby reached out for help, Mike O'brien was on the phone holding a confidential file labeled MARK HALLY.

"Good Morning Mike thanks for getting back so quick."

"No problem Tony that's what I get paid for," hesitating for a moment Mike continued, "Do you want the good news or bad news first." Tony anxiously laughed,

"Let's look behind door number 2 first - what's the down side?"

"Well for starters, most of his public files are missing and that's unusual….based on a preliminary review I'd say they've been expunged."

"Can he do that?" "Not from the sources we dig into, this would have had to be done by someone with enough juice to cut across several Government agencies; I'm impressed, haven't seen this since the cold war days."

"What else Mike?"

"His personal files are typical, nothing unusual, pretty smart guy though, his name popped up as a contributing author on several major academic studies, what did you say his job was?"

"Draftsman," Tony intently replied, Mike laughed,

"No way Tony this guy is a valuable asset."

"Yea, well lucky me I got him cheap….thanks Mike, that tells me what I need to know."

Chapter 8

THE WORLD TURNED UPSIDE DOWN

Bob Tosky was carefully reviewing progress and the schedule needed to safely make a return trip from Mars. Well aware that Industry and Government eyes were now focused on the viability of the program, his reputation, personal fortune and the lives of the crew hung in the balance. Things had gone better than expected up to the landing and the prospect of a team mole sabotaging the program with Alpha's extensive protocols in place defied credibility. How this could happen was no longer an issue in his mind, only the return trip and Tosky was determined to make sure his team was ready to get it done.

"Where do we stand today," he sternly asked Alpha's flight team, adding "I want details... what are we still looking at?"

"Bob the recovery ship is still being fitted out," the flight director explained, "we've verified Jay Lanza's virus discovery and are checking out the programming patch he made for the navigation software as we speak; you do know that as of the last communication D'Antonio wants to return in Horizon 1, said the ship will be ready in a few days."

"For Christ sake," Tosky blurted out, "Horizon 1 crashed landed, who the hell knows what damage the ship sustained." Banging his fist on the conference room table he yelled, "Remind Mr. D'Antonio flight decisions are made down here, it's not a field decision and ITS NOT NEGOTIABLE - I repeat, NOT NEGOTIABLE." Tosky was still hot under the collar when he called ArmorTec. "Tony its Bob, what the hell are we doing about our mole?"

"Easy Bob, we still need to confirm our suspicions; I want to build a technical and financial case before I make any accusations."

"Well I suggest you put it into high gear buddy, your boss is planning a return trip in Horizon 1."

"What?" Tony asked in a surprised tone; "when is he returning, and why the hell are you authorizing Horizon 1?"

"I didn't" Tosky angrily replied, "but you know D'Antonio, I'm not sure I can stop him…we need to come up with a damn good reason to postpone the trip and we need it soon."

"Son of a Bitch," I growled, when Alpha's communication order was received cancelling Horizon 1's return. "What the hell do they want us to do, drop dead waiting for the Calvary to arrive?"

"Probably just being cautious," Phil surmised.

"CAUTION MY ASS, their caution almost got us killed….I guess they forgot the abort decision they dumped in my lap; believe me, Tosky would rather see us rot up here than risk another crash. Look we have all the data needed to make the trip. Besides we have a man down and a prolonged stay in this condition can be a bigger danger - no, I say we go."

"All right Tom you're still the captain, whatever you decide is OK with me but it may be a life and death decision, and I think we should hear from the rest of the crew." The crew members were somber after learning of the return flight postponement order from flight control. The delay could be extensive and most of the scheduled activities for the mission were now complete. The psychological impact of isolation and boredom would be bad enough and adding in concerns over limited life support and the same mundane food supply may be intolerable. I never imagined eating the same damn yogurt like rations week after week could be so depressing. I began having nightmares over it and I was sure the rest of the crew felt the same way.

"All right ladies and gentlemen," I said, "listen up, you know the choices - we either wait for Lazarus or take control of our own fate - what say you?" Hodges and Larson were adamant they were ready to go.

"Tom there's absolutely no reason to wait," John Hodges spoke up, "the ship's structure is intact and all systems are completely serviceable except for the hydraulic landing pods."

"Yea and that shouldn't be a problem," Hank Larson added, "as long as we have a controlled slow speed touchdown." Lillian Banks hollered out

"Hopefully slower than the last one Hank," we all laughed and Lillian continued, "I'm not sure I could handle a repeat episode, are we sure the bug is gone?" "The system is clean" Jay Lanza immediately replied in a confident tone,

"We've run 3 successful return simulations."

"OK sounds like it's unanimous," I said, "looks like we're a go."

"Hold on Tom," Sue Lee interrupted, "Jim and I aren't going anywhere even if Jim survived the trip a return to Earth's gravity would kill him."

"How can you be so sure?"

"Oh I'm sure," Sue firmly replied, "had it confirmed by the Neurology Department at Johns Hopkins and you can't get more definitive than that. He has a spinal fracture at his C2 and C3 discs. The reduced gravity is keeping him alive; any added pressure could pinch off or sever the nerve controlling his breathing resulting in immediate suffocation."

"No other options?" I quietly asked,

"That's it in a nut shell, C2 and C3 must be fused to stabilize the spinal column and that has to be done by an experienced neurosurgeon." Confronted with the facts of Jim's situation and Sue's determination I was taken back with admiration and momentarily a bit of jealousy. Walking over to Sue I said

"that kind of love deserves all the help that's in my power. I promise you we'll come back and Jim's care will be a top priority on the next mission."

With a renewed sense of urgency Tony Colby was determined to fast track his investigation. Joe Campo and Marie arrived early Saturday morning after a late night call from Tony.

"All right what's the emergency?" Joe demanded walking into the conference room. Seated at the back of the room a tall burly man got up and introduced himself -

"Mike Obrien Joe, glad to finally meet you." Joe gasped in surprise,

"MIKE, Mike Obrien, I never did get a chance to thank you for saving my ass" while vigorously shaking his hand and giving him a bear-hug.

"OK, OK you two can dance later," Tony interrupted. "We've got a lot of work to do and no time to do it." Tony continued explaining the situation on Mars and at mission control. When he finished the room was silent for a moment.

"What did you have in mind Tony?" Mike asked.

"That's what I was going to ask you, how do we smoke this rat out; can't be obvious, if we confront him directly we won't get to the truth any time soon."

"I've done some snooping into his financial records," Joe added; "for a working stiff he has some unusual accounts."

"Like what?" Tony asked.

"He has a standard checking and savings account at a local bank, nothing special, but he has 2 off-shore accounts - one in Belize and the other in Zurich. I can't get at the Zurich account without a Government order but my contact in Belize should have something today." Mike stood up pacing the floor,

"The easiest way to get to the truth is by looking for lies, and that means a polygraph test."

"Yea… but why would he consent to a test?" Joe asked, "and not get suspicious."

"Reminds me of an investigation I did for a munitions company," Mike replied. "They suspected someone had sabotaged a critical 20mm production line during the Iraq war days by slipping a solid steel blank into a brass cupping line smashing tools and putting the press out of commission;

to keep it covert we tested the entire production crew, told them it was a new employment requirement imposed by the Government for security purposes."

"Maybe Mike," Tony interrupted, "but he's still going to suspect something's up."

"Doesn't matter Tony all we have to do is get him to take the test. Once we're into it we'll pick out the lies, even if he refuses to answer some of the questions and then we'll break him down." After listening to the story Marie innocently asked,

"Did you get the guy Mike?"

"I got the bastard" he replied, Tony smiled at his friend, reassured that if anybody could get to the bottom of this Obrien was the man, and in a decisive tone said,

"OK, let's do it, it's the best idea, correction the only idea we have."

Harry Perot had spent the last week exploring every avenue he knew to break thru the bureaucratic maze at Missile Command. The clues and bits of communications he managed to squeeze out of lower level contacts regarding the DREAM propulsion system and the Sioux involvement always led down a blind alley. Nothing, he thought, it's really odd not even a rumor although he instinctively knew that the information he needed was out of standard communication protocols; this would have been a "for your eyes only" document and hidden within the highest management levels. Frustrated and at a loss where to go next he began to realize the futility of his efforts and his own arrogance in believing he could break thru this kind of security by himself. Packing for his trip back to the launch facility in South Dakota, his cell phone rang,

"Hello Mr. Perot" an unfamiliar voice came on, "I understand you've been asking some, shall we say, very unusual questions at the Command."

"Who the hell is this?" Harry demanded –

"A friend Mr. Perot, a friend." An hour later Harry hurriedly finished packing and called to change his flight reservations – he knew what had to be done now and was not going to make the same mistake again. South Dakota could wait; he had 45 minutes to catch a red eye flight to New Jersey.

The Mars landing zone, now named Oglala Station in honor of the Sioux Nation, was put into top operating condition to ensure life support services to home base, in preparation for our departure. Vehicles were fully fueled and parked alongside the egress platform although Sunday drives were not expected except for some unforeseen emergency. The nuclear generator and drilling units were carefully inspected and serviced along with the hydrogen, oxygen and water storage tanks. During our departure these systems were designed to automatically replenish themselves and provide a continuous supply to home base with minimal maintenance. To ensure this a constant flow of water from the ice pack was allowed by programming a minimal demand requirement into the operating software. Under this format half the water volume is diverted to the electrolysis unit and broken down into its Hydrogen and Oxygen components. Any overflow H_2O is collected in an open detention basin which quickly evaporates due to the thin Martian atmosphere. Similarly any excess hydrogen or oxygen beyond the pressure tanks 50 psi thresholds is vented to the atmosphere. Of course in this case, any maintenance would have to be performed by Sue; she was smart and knew how to handle tools, plus our cross training in preparation for the mission was now paying off. My only concern was her physical capability; she was petite in a word and I was intimately aware of the physical effort needed to work outside the shelter. In any event Sue and Jim Dougherty could sustain themselves on the planet for over a year, if needed, with minimal maintenance although our expectations for a return amounted to a few months, but first de-coupling from home base had to be done and preparations were now on schedule for an early morning launch.

Sitting in his office Marie's voice came over the intercom,

"Ok Mark it's your turn, the test people are waiting for you in the conference room."

"Be right there Marie," Hally replied, apparently oblivious to the sting operation now set in motion.

"Good morning Mr. Hally," Mike Obrien greeted in a pleasant voice, "please take a seat here," pointing to a table with a maze of sensors and recording equipment. "I'll just wire you up and we can begin." Hally nodded casually and sat down.

"Sure this won't hurt?" he asked and nervously laughed.

"Nothing to it, I'll just ask you a few simple questions to establish a personal response baseline and please reply with direct answers; you don't have to elaborate, understood?"

"Got it," Hally replied in a shrill tone of voice.

"OK let's begin - is your name Mark Hally?"

"Yes."

"Is your street address 104 Independence court?"

"Yes"…..

"Do you work for ArmorTec as a draftsman?" Again the reply was yes as the simple questions began to be more involved. Another 15 minutes went by and Mike looked up,

"that's it Mr. Hally, you're all through."

"Did I pass?" Hally asked standing up.

"It's not that kind of test," Mike replied.

"No I mean, can I still work at ArmorTec?" Hally nervously persisted.

"That's not up to me; you'll get a post-test interview after we analyze the data."

Tony Colby was impatiently pacing the floor in his office when Mike's voice came over the intercom.

"Tony come on in, the interview is over." Walking into the conference room Tony was bursting with anticipation.

"Did you get the son of a bitch?….break him down did you- Did he confess?"

"Not exactly Tony, we have some unexpected results. Your Mr. Hally is a real cool cucumber. He's either the best professional liar I've ever come across or he's completely innocent."

"I don't get it Mike?" Tony asked in an exasperated voice - "it all fit, how the hell could it not be him?"

"I got nothing on him Tony, look at his reactions"… pointing to a recording section; "here… I asked him if he ever divulged any technical information to anyone outside of ArmorTec; his reply was no and his reaction was no different than his response to his name or address." Tony was livid now, pressing the intercom he hollered,

"Marie, tell Mark Hally to get back in here immediately and ask Joe Campo to come in."

"What are you doing Tony?" Mike asked in surprise.

"Sorry buddy, I've got to get to the bottom of this, by God even if I have to beat it out of him." Walking into the conference room Mark Hally couldn't help noticing the somber faces gathered around the conference table.

"This looks serious gentlemen," Hally said in a resigned voice, "is this about my test results?" Tony went right for the jugular.

"Is there something you want to tell us Mark... why are you lying about your credential? - you're no draftsman." A dead silence came over the room while Hally tried to compose himself. Looking up he began to quietly talk.

"I was afraid it would come to this, it always comes back like a bad headache - how did you find out?"

"Find out, FIND OUT," Tony shouted while standing up; "you almost got an entire crew killed, not to mention ruining a multi-billion dollar mission you bastard."

"Now hold on, HOLD ON," Hally yelled back with a confused look on his face. "What the hell are you talking about?"

"Don't give me that bullshit," Tony yelled, "you know damn well what we're talking about... sabotage..... The software virus you installed in the ships computer." Hally fell back in his chair.

"Mr. Colby you've got the wrong guy, I never touched the mission software." Mike Obrien held his hand up,

"Mark, what did you think we found out?" Hally took a deep breath and replied

"My discharge from the NSA."

"I KNEW IT, I KNEW YOU WERE A MOLE," Tony screamed.

"Easy Tony," Mike interrupted, "let him finish - go on Mark."

"I use to be a senior program administrator for the NSA; a couple of years ago as part of intelligence surveillance authorized by the Patriot Act, private phone records and emails were being reviewed. It was all standard activity in the beginning and then gradually, the program started to spin out of control. Specific groups were being targeted for political reasons and I objected and eventually threatened to go public with these abuses. That was a mistake, I would have been better off being a whistle blower but my loyalties took over, thought I could help change the culture. In any event, management jumped on it, and began prosecuting me on trumped up conspiracy charges. In the end I cut a deal; had my background records expunged and was prohibited from programming work for any Government project or agency."

When he finished Tony starred silently in disbelief.

"If I was wrong Mark I apologize - but how do you explain the offshore bank accounts?"

"Mr. Colby, before I cut a deal I expected to be a fugitive, and rather than spending the next 20 years rotting in a Federal prison I was prepared to repatriate to a foreign country; it seemed like the only way I could keep the feds from confiscating my money." Joe Campo nodded his head and added

"Makes sense Tony; both accounts aren't active."

"If that's the case we still have a problem," Tony said, "there's still a mole out there trying to screw things up."

"Look, I spent a lot of years creating and tracking down viruses for the NSA" Mark interrupted, "maybe I could help? - do you have a technical description of the virus, or better yet if I could look at the software?"

"We do and you could," Tony replied, "but first I'm gonna check out your story with the NSA; I still have contacts there."

"Be my guest Mr. Colby; I suggest you start with the Criminal Justice Division, those records should still be intact."

Bob Tosky was a superb administrator and allowed his staff to run their own show. Walking into Alpha's headquarters located a short drive from Philly International, Harry Perot also knew his boss wanted first-hand information, good or bad, in person and critical decisions were his and his alone.

"Good morning Betsy," Harry said smiling "is the boss in?"

"Why Mr. Perot, what a pleasant surprise I'll let him know you're here." A few minutes later Bob Tosky strolled out of his office greeting Harry,

"Thought you were still in South Dakota."

"Change of plans Bob, I wanted to let you know the outcome of the Tribes facility funding problem."

"Sure, Harry," Tosky replied walking back to his office; "I'll have some coffee sent in and you can tell me all about it." Harry stared at his boss briefly, wondering how he would react to the bomb he was about to drop in his lap. "Harry I know about the Tribes concern over the loss of Grant funding; it's not a big deal, we can replace the money while they fight that battle with DIA…. we can bring a lot of pressure to bear and I'm sure they'll be able to overturn that decision."

"That's great Bob, but this thing has legs and there are some other complicating issues we may have to deal with."

"Go on, you have my attention," Tosky said, noticing the concern on Harry's face.

"As you know my contacts at Homeland Security led me to Missile Command. After a full week of probing I came up with nothing, until I got a call from a very, very well informed individual,"

"And who was that?"

"Don't know Bob, wouldn't tell me his name, but I can tell you he must have been involved in the Sioux decision."

"How do you know?" "Because only someone part of the Government's intelligence machinery could have known the details he provided; he was legit Bob, I'm sure." Harry continued for over an hour describing a plot to terminate ArmorTec's Martian program at any cost. Apparently initiated by an Aerospace conglomerate petitioning a group of Senators to cancel Tribal funding, the original intent got distorted going thru covert Government agencies, finally winding up at NSA with orders to make the program go away. "Missile Command had the assets to discretely accomplish the mission," Harry explained, "and with the help of NSA put a covert team together, reporting to…. you're not gonna believe this…. the Administration's point man for campaign contributions. A classic case of, I think the military term is, Cluster Fuck." Tosky sat back in his chair stunned.

"They can't get away with this, they won't get away with this and if they think they've covered their asses they're in for a big surprise." Red faced now Tosky was venting; he understood the implications and the threat to his personal fortune. "I'm calling the press, television stations anybody in the media….." Listening to the 10 - minute tirade, Harry patiently waited for Tosky to calm down.

"Whatever you say Bob, but don't you think a direct accusation will bring a concerted Government denial? The bastards are good at that, maybe we should hit them where they least expect it." Tosky paused, looking at Harry for a few moments and grinned.

"You're trying to sell a salesman Harry, drop the sales pitch, what did you have in mind?"

It was Saturday and the early morning traffic driving to ArmorTec's offices was light. The past week was a blur of activity and disappointment working 12-hour days and the casual trip to the office afforded Tony Colby some rare down time. He never bargained for this much activity; it's a younger man's job he thought, someone not concerned about blood pressure, indigestion or back pain just getting out of bed but he knew full well a fire burned in his belly; he had to go on no matter what, like everyone else he was hooked - Mars was calling. Arriving at the office Mark Hally was already there. Tony verified his story the previous day and released the entire software program, including the patch created by Jay Lanza and Stage 5 telemetry for the flight of Horizon 1. Mark went at it the same day and hadn't stopped for 48 hours straight.

The Martian sunrise was just coming up as the Horizon crew intently began a countdown for de-coupling from home base. Our pilot Hank Larson was scheduled to execute the maneuver by himself, a short 60 second flight slowly lifting the command and second stage modules 50 feet up and landing 100 feet outside of our base perimeter and original landing site. The Nav computer was pre-programmed to autonomously perform the flight and Larson was there as a redundancy if any unexpected adjustments were required. Part of our communication equipment was relocated to home base to function as a real time mission control relay station and would be retained there for the staff left behind in our absence.

"All systems are a go," Hank Larson's voice snapped over the Intercom.

"That's affirm," John Hodges replied, "still setting up telemetry tracking Hank, should be ready within the hour."

"Copy that John," Larson replied in a relaxed tone, "just wake me up when you're ready."

"Ready for a break?" Tony Colby asked, walking into Mark Hally's office.

"Oh Hi, Mr. Colby almost, just organizing my thoughts. Pretty nasty stuff; your Jay Lanza's a real pro, did a hell of a job locating that bug."

"Yea we're lucky to have him, anything else pop out at you?"

"Not really, I only focused on the bug and patch that Lanza made. It's not a unique virus, in fact it's very similar to some of the bugs we developed at NSA; if I had to guess I would say its origin, at least the prototype version is definitely Government, not commercial."

"That's interesting, you sure about that?"

"Almost positive," Hally replied, "you see the coding protocols are organized in a very specific way; we did that in order to identify and keep track of our own work, something a freelance hacker would never do. There's something I must have missed in the patch though; if memory serves me, this particular bug had, what we use to call a Little Sister, a built in redundancy."

"Mark go slow here, you're losing me…and this Little Sister does what?" Tony nervously asked.

"The same thing the primary bug does; when the bug is extracted it unsuspectingly launches a Little Sister back into the software; it's a secondary time bomb." The blood immediately drained from Tony's face. Frozen for a moment he gasped.

"My God man, Horizon 1 is scheduled for a lift off this morning; are you telling me Lanza's patch is wrong?"

"Looks that way Mr. Colby." Tony stood up in a panic and ran down the hall to the satellite telecommunication link.

"MARIE, MARIE, QUICK WE'VE GOT TO GET A MESSAGE TO TOM RIGHT NOW."

"OK Hank, you can wake up now, time to get back in the saddle," John Hodges voice pierced the silence in the command module.

"That's affirmative John, ready when you are." We're setting the launch clock at 10 minutes to lift off; mission control wants you to go thru your checklist again."

"Copy that John, systems check list repeat confirmed." Glancing over at me I nodded at Hodges; nodding back he touched the chronometer while confirming, "Set Your Mark…. 10 minutes and counting - the clock has started." Larson was incredible - how the hell does he remain so calm? I thought. I'm not on the ship and my hands are sweating.

"Four minutes and counting," Hodges voice echoed snapping me back to reality.

"Copy that," Larson casually replied, "all systems are go." In the meantime I kept thinking about the trip home; I was feeling isolated and wanted to see familiar things again, my Condo, my office and friends back on earth, green grass and blue sky and eat a steak dinner at my favorite restaurant. All these thoughts kept rushing in, over and over again and today would be my last day on Mars. The thought gave me a dull ache in my stomach. Mars was my Mistress, and now it was time to go. Again Hodges voice rang out counting,

"ten, nine" as Lillian Banks interrupted my concentration.

"Tom we're getting a priority message from Tony Colby."

"Hold on Lillian", I said as the ship lifted off.

"It's one word," Lillian urgently persisted.

"What, What is it?"

"ABORT" she replied in a surprised tone of voice. Abort, ABORT I thought, the word struck me like a fist; the ship was now at altitude and beginning to traverse out of our perimeter. Grabbing Hodge's head set I stuttered in a panic.

"Hank, HANK, put the ship on the ground immediately;" as the words left my mouth, the sound of Hank Larson's voice groaned as the ship nose-dived crashing into the Martian surface.

"Did we have a clear line Marie?" Tony Colby anxiously asked.

"The transmission went thru uninterrupted, but we'll have to wait another 8 minutes to get confirmation." Colby paced the floor in his office waiting for a reply as Marie walked in visibly shaken.

"The ship crashed Tony!"

"Oh my God, can any other fucking thing go wrong," he yelled looking at her.

"Yes," she sobbed, "Hank Larson was killed in the crash." The news hit Bob Tosky's office at the same time, like an earthquake the entire staff rumbled around for a few minutes in shock and then busily started analyzing telemetry, putting the crash forensics pieces together. Tosky was fuming inside, but years of business experience taught him to face the facts and not look back. He had to rearrange the program now, rescue the stranded crew on Mars, and do it all, while out-maneuvering NSA, the Justice Department, and competing Aerospace companies. Although Lazarus was almost ready for a rescue mission, the technical challenges that posed a danger were nothing compared to the invisible threat posed by the Government and that had to be dealt with first.

Hank Larson's body was retrieved from the wreckage and placed in a body bag alongside a makeshift grave dug

100 yards from the crash site. His neck was broken but otherwise his body showed no evidence of a fatal crash, bad luck I wondered or simply a result of my own ego and hard headedness; either way Mars had its first casualty….Jay Lanza felt personally responsible and at first was inconsolable. I thought he was trying to kill himself watching him bang his head against the bulkhead when he learned of the flaw in his patch. It took two of us to restrain him and a sedative injected by Sue Lee before he calmed down. A full day had passed as we assessed the damage to the command module and prepared Hank's body for burial. The ships controls and power panels were a mangled mess along with the Nav Computer. We were stranded now and our fate was irretrievably in the hands of mission control and a rescue mission. In the end Tosky got his wish I thought but I would have given anything, even my life, to have it otherwise. At noon the next day the entire crew with the exception of Jim Dougherty suited up and drove to the grave site for a burial service. As Captain I was expected to preside over the service, but my guilt over the accident hung on my shoulders so that I could barely speak.

"Hank we're all here to say goodbye," I said in a woeful voice, "and to let you know how sorry we are that you're gone. You won't be forgotten buddy." After an awkward pause Lillian Banks spoke up.

"We will meet again, in God's good time, until then may he receive your soul and bless you, in the name of the Father, the Son and the Holy Ghost." As we left the grave I couldn't help thinking, Christ lived on earth, but for the first time I began to understand the meaning of his universal spirit having felt his presence on Mars.

Bob Tosky remained stoic as he listened to Harry Perot's plan to neutralize the Governments covert operation to terminate the Mars program. It was a masterful idea. He was impressed and thankful that one of his employees was that insightful and committed to the company.

"It's clear to me," Harry went on, "these boys want and need inside information to shut us down and we're at a disadvantage since we don't know how or when they'll attack. So we have to change the rules of the game; instead of relying on our internal security, which seems to be flawed let's give them what they want and wait for a reaction, only this time we would know where and when." Tosky smiled, and said,

"You mean a sting operation."

"Sort of, if you know someone is about to commit a crime the simple solution is to call a cop."

"Yes but these snakes are the cops," Tosky interrupted.

"Only one of the cops, corrupt cops," Harry continued, "if we can smoke them out and have a good cop catch them perpetrating a crime we'll have the credibility and advantage using our publicity assets to take them down."

"I like it Harry, it's a clean idea, and as of right now I'm making all of our resources available to you to make this happen."

"Hold on Bob," Harry replied in a surprised tone of voice. "This is way over my head; I don't have the experience to pull this off."

"You're doing fine Harry and don't worry, you'll have plenty of help but for now you're the point man, I want you to start right away, the lives of a crew on Mars are at stake."

With a select team of Alpha employees now at his disposal, Harry wasted no time putting his plan in motion. No one, absolutely no one other than Bob Tosky and Tony Colby was to know anything about the misinformation about to be transmitted throughout the organization.

"Good morning Tony," Harry's voice came on.

"Hey Harry haven't seen you in a while, what's up?"

"Tony I'm stationed at Alpha's offices now and I need you for a meeting here today."

"Sorry my schedule's full buddy, I have an important 2 o'clock." Before Colby could finish Harry cut in.

"Tony this is top priority, the boss wants us to schedule a rapid deployment recovery mission."

"Harry, you know as well as me, we're not ready yet." Again Harry interrupted.

"Listen Tony, the picture has changed, things have deteriorated on Mars and the crew is now in imminent danger, please don't argue with me, just get over here and I'll fill you in." Twenty minutes later sitting in Perot's office Colby patiently listened to Harry's plan code named Angel Fire, under the pretext of an emergency recovery mission.

"Tony we're going to make this real, right up to the launch."

"It's going to cost a boat load of money Harry and we're simply going to throw it down the toilet? If you give it to me, I'll make sure they wouldn't get within a hundred miles of our launch pad and we'll get the crew back safe and sound."

"Tony we both know these guys won't stop even if we could launch a secure mission, they'll be back and sooner or later we'll have a disaster on our hands, probably lose the whole damn program. No, we stop them now before anything else happens."

"Alright we'll do it your way. But promise me one thing Harry, if Tom and his crew really are at risk we'll take our chances and get them back."

"Sure Tony, but first we've got to give Angel Fire a chance."

Within one week Angel Fire details were firmly put in place while Alpha's launch team working 24/7 rolled out Lazarus on the launch pad in South Dakota. All the gear and equipment needed for the flight were in transit and the ship was scheduled for full fit out within 3 days. The sabotage of Horizon1's software, now out in the open, was no longer considered an option and any covert attack would have to occur at the launch pad prior to Stage 1, near earth flight. Alpha and ArmorTec employees were discretely notified of the impending flight and security at the launch pad appeared normal, even lax, disguising the full time electronic surveillance now in place, and the quick response teams hidden and bivouacked on site. The crime scene was ready, waiting for a crook and a cop to show up.

Although he had serious reservations about Angel Fire Tony Colby was committed and prepared to do his part. At ArmorTec he alone knew the real purpose of Angel Fire and openly conveyed a false sense of enthusiasm for the rescue mission. Time was now running out and it was his responsibility to put the final piece of the sting in place. Brett Allen had just arrived at his office at the Justice Department in DC, when his secretary waived to him getting off the elevator.

"Good morning Brett, a Mr. Colby from ArmorTec called, said it was urgent that he speak with you today."

"Thanks Carla I've been meaning to get in touch with him, please get him on the phone and transfer the call to my office." A few moments later the call came thru.

"Hello Colonel Colby, Brett Allen here, I'm returning your call."

"Good morning Brett, I called to give you an update on the DREAM personnel you want to interview for the Eminent Domain order," Allen paused for a moment, suspicious of the cooperation offered.

"Sure Colonel I'm all ears, where are they?"

"Unfortunately still on Mars Brett, but we're scheduling a rescue mission this week."

"I heard that thru the rumor mill Tony didn't think it was true, but thanks for the confirmation."

"Brett I know we got off on the wrong foot but I want you to know we're ready to play ball."

"Why the change of heart Tony?"

"Listen Brett, you were right the first time we talked, I was a Colonel in the United States Air Force and I am a patriot. I probably understand better than you the consequences of DREAM falling into the wrong hands…. besides we could use your help."

Lift off was a day away and mission control was straining to complete all of the pre-flight checks, cargo inspections and crew accommodations; weeks of normal launch activities now compressed into days had CAPCOM personnel on edge over concerns to get it right the first time. Bob Tosky had personally informed them of the emergency, implying that any minor glitches, not affecting the safety of the crew should not be a cause for delay or reason to scrub the mission. Senior management personnel were now arguing trying to explain to nervous flight personnel the interpretation of a minor glitch; aware of the confusion spreading thru the team the flight director intervened.

"People I want everyone to settle down and man your post; we'll address anything that comes up one issue at a time, just flag it and continue working the program. We have a ship to get off the ground in less than 24 hours."

Relentless activity at Mission Control continued well into the night. The ship was ready now and except for a skeleton maintenance crew all flight personnel had vacated the building. A bright moonlit sky eerily reflected the ship's shadow on the launch pad, serene and motionless, except for the imperceptible motion of the scanning video units, disguised as light fixtures. A mile away buried in command bunkers, Justice Department counter insurgency teams were busily monitoring any activity around the launch pad ready to move out at a moment's notice. The first alert came in at 1:00 AM as response team members scrambled for their gear and lined up in a hallway at bunker exits. The lead elements of each team would drive directly to the launch site while the remaining members were expected to fan out on foot in a perimeter and sweep into the launch pad, restraining anyone or anything encountered. Everyone was staring at the two lights mounted over the exit, a green for go and a red for abort; five endless minutes passed in total silence when the red light flashed on.

"All right pack it in, it's a false alarm," the squad leader in alpha bunker said in a resigned tone of voice, "everybody stay alert, we're gonna do this right thru the night." Another abort occurred a half hour later prompting team commanders to request visual confirmation before an alert. Up till then any movement initiated an alert, the first was a herd of deer darting across the launch pad and the second an Indian guard running to the weeds to take a leak. Shortly after, a third alert was signaled and simultaneously a voice from the monitoring crew hollered,

"I have visual confirmation, repeat visual confirmation," as the green go light flashed, adding "one guard down, another guard down and multiple bogies running on site." In a blur of activity lead team members in Humvees converged on the launch pad in seconds, as the bunkers emptied out scattering men in a semicircle around the launch pad. Now running, peering thru night vision binoculars, nothing inside would or could escape as the human net closed. Surprising the insurgents the lead teams arriving on site were met with small arms fire. A half dozen bogies were crouched down near the ship firing automatic weapons forcing the Humvees occupants from the south side to unload and set up a skirmishing line returning fire. One of the Humvees approaching from the north managed to move in close from the opposite side of the ship, rendering the bogies position untenable. Watching the bogies retreat now, Alpha team's squad leader hollered

"CHARGE," while standing up, "LETS GET THE BASTARDS." Closing in on their retreating targets, rapid fire flashes suddenly appeared from a tree line along the perimeter gate as the squad leader watched in horror, several of his men go down. Realizing his mistake they were now caught out in the open in a deadly covering fire from expert marksmen in entrenched positions. Waving his arms and yelling at his men, "TAKE COVER, BACK TO THE VEHICLE," the squad began retreating. Noticing some movement he stopped and picked up one of the wounded; barely running now 10 feet from the vehicle a single shot ripped thru the man on his back and exited thru the front of his chest. Dropping like a pair of marionettes, both men were dead.

Monitoring the situation in South Dakota, Tosky, Perot and Tony Colby, were huddled around a video terminal viewing the gun battle going on. The retreating bogies under the cover fire of snipers ran toward the perimeter gate, away from the oncoming semicircle of troops. Unaware that several squads of Indian guards were hidden in the brush parallel to and outside the gate, their escape route was now compromised. A fierce fire fight immediately broke out as the Sioux warriors mounted a head on charge and despite a withering repelling fire, engaged in hand to hand combat. At the same time on rushing insurgency teams overwhelmed the position forcing the bogies to drop their weapons and surrender. The whole battle lasted less than 10 minutes, but despite the short duration and intense planning the kill rate was high. Out of a total of 12 bogies, 6 were killed, 3 wounded and 3 taken into custody. The Sioux lost 7 warriors and 8 critically wounded. The advance elements of the insurgency teams fared the worst; 10 men were killed in the initial cover fire and 12 wounded mainly from friendly fire in the chaos of the attack; but the conflict was over and Tosky breathed a sigh of relief.

"Harry I want you to leave tonight for South Dakota," he said in a firm tone of voice, "a company jet is waiting for you at the airport; we have another mission to get ready for."

The highways leading to the reservation were empty at 5 AM in the morning and although the tension of the past few hours had physically exhausted him, an adrenaline rush was keeping Harry Perot alert. Arriving at the flight facility, ambulances and EMTs were still on site tagging body bags and attending to the walking wounded. He quickly found Brett Allen at a makeshift office at the launch pad, interviewing his men for a post mission report.

"Brett, Brett Allen, glad you're OK," Harry called out waving his arm, "watched the whole damn thing on television."

"Hi Harry, yea just like a video game except we lost a lot of good men."

"Sorry Brett"….Harry paused for a moment, "I know how hard that is, but we still have to get to the bottom of this; do you have any Intel on the prisoners yet."

"Not much Harry, these guys are pro's, they shut down tighter than a crabs ass."

"Where are they now?" Harry asked.

"The Sioux have them in a lock up; we had a hard time convincing them they were valuable intelligence assets, wanted to kill them right after they surrendered. By the way you're the Indian expert, what the hell is a Spirit Dance?" Harry stared at Allen for a moment as the hint of a grin came on his face.

"Why do you ask?"

"They told me it was something they wanted to try, said it was a purifying ritual."

"Let them do it Brett, it's probably our only shot at a confession."

Arriving at ArmorTec late that morning, Tony Colby was surprisingly calm, the sting worked, he thought, and despite the loss of life this whole sordid affair was coming to an end.

"Good Morning," Marie cheerfully said as he walked into the office, "we all heard the good news Tony, congratulations."

"Thanks Marie, just glad it's all over."

"You have company," Marie added, "Mike O'Brien is here, he's been waiting for you since 9 o'clock." Walking into the conference room Mike Obrien was sitting down staring at the contents of a manila folder.

"Hi Mike, thought you were back in DC."

"I was Tony but I wanted you to see this."

"Sounds serious Mike."

"It is Tony, please sit down." O'Brien went on, "as a precaution I had your phones tapped after the polygraph tests; didn't think you would mind."

"Sure Mike, what did you find?"

"Some very interesting, to put it mildly, calls that Joe Campo had." After reading the transcripts Tony remained motionless, the dialogue was damaging and undeniable, including several conversations with operatives from the NSA.

An old teepee - like structure stood menacingly in a remote field on the Sioux reservation. Nearby large wood burning boilers were smoking feeding scalding water and steam into the lodge. Worn foot paths leading to and from the structure were evident of its long use where Indian boys began their journey. An ancient Sioux ceremony, known as the Spirit Dance transformed boys into Sioux Braves by enduring the trials of this rite of passage. Each of the insurgent prisoners, bound with hoods over their heads was led into the lodge. The sauna like atmosphere inside was stifling to the uninitiated immediately producing beads of sweat as the prisoners were stripped to their waists. Outside screams were audible as large talon like hooks were dug deep into their chest muscles used as body attachments for the overhead hoists that would raise their bodies. Slowly, as the attending guard pulled the hoist line the chest muscles deformed swelling up until their feet left the ground. Now dangling there any bodily movement would cause excruciating pain and there they would remain amid the smoke and heat until the Indian Shaman was sure the Spirit Dance exacted the truth. Within 24 hours all 3 prisoners now transformed, separately signed confessions attesting to the attack and identifying their chain of command. Transferring the prisoners to local authorities, Brett Allen shook his head,

"Harry if I hadn't seen this with my own eyes, I'd say you were crazy; someday you'll tell me how they did this."

"It's a secret Brett, besides, you really don't want to know."

Chapter 9
PROMISES KEPT

The mood at Alpha headquarters dramatically changed as Bob Tosky planned to press his advantage and expose the covert Government organizations that had threatened the Mars program, his personal fortune and the lives of his employees. A list of media moguls and press releases were being prepared when a call from the Department of Justice came in.

"Hello Bob, its Brett Allen."

"I see you made it back safe and sound Brett. You did a real service for the country, now what can I do for you?"

"Bob you do know I want to take down the bastards behind this as much as you," Tosky quickly cut in,

"No Brett, not as much, not anywhere near as much, I want them gone never to threaten anyone again."

"All right, all right," Allen laughed nervously, "not as much as you, but what would you say if we went after the people actively involved? I assure you they would never see the light of day."

"Sure that's a start, go get em tiger."

"Well not a start Bob it's more like an end." Tosky caught by surprise, paused trying to grasp the implications.

"If you're telling me you'll take down the clowns they cut loose without touching the puppet masters that's bullshit buddy."

"Not at all Bob," "Allen cautiously replied, "we'll get the bastards who planned this to."

"Oh yea, just like that, and what on this screwed up earth would make me believe that?"

"Look Bob, nobody's going to get a free ride. We just can't afford to completely disrupt critical Government agencies that manage our National Security; the administration won't allow it."

"THE ADMINISTRATION," Tosky hollered, "for Christ's sake their culpable to."

"Only one delusional man Bob, and he's already gone, the president's chief of staff demanded his resignation this morning and charges are being brought as we speak."

"And that's supposed to make me feel good," Tosky gasped in disbelief.

"Bob you don't know it yet but you've already won; the administration understands the repercussions this could have and they know you could hurt them politically; I've been authorized to offer you substantial concessions regarding the Eminent Domain order in recognition of course, of your contributions to science and technology, and I'm sure you do realize how nasty things could get if you turn them down."

"Of Course," Tosky cynically replied, "and what are these concessions?"

"Although we still have the right to make use or buy for national security purposes, you will retain unlimited commercial licensing rights, including foreign Governments on our free trade list. Again in recognition of your contributions, your company will be the US Governments sole source contractor for delivery of any DREAM vehicles over the next 5 years with access to any Government facility assets and financing, that's it in a nut shell." Allen took a deep breath and stopped talking, trying to assess Tosky's reaction. A long pause came between the men.

"That's quite an offer," Tosky finally said in a casual tone of voice, "give me a day to think about it."

Tony Colby had disappeared for a few days trying to come to grips with the apparent treachery of his friend; his mind constantly wavering between convictions of his guilt one moment and plausible excuses the next. By the second day, thinking about it had emotionally drained him and yet, hoping for the best he feared the outcome of his next meeting with Joe Campo.

"Good morning Joe," Marie casually said, while sorting the day's mail, "Tony's here, said he wanted to see you today." Walking into his office Joe couldn't help noticing the dark circles under Tony's eyes.

"Where the hell have you been," Joe unsuspectingly said. "You look like hell."

"Feel like it too," Tony replied, staring at his friend. "Joe sit down, I want you to read these transcripts."

"What are they Tony?" "Copies of telephone conversations Mike O'Brien secretly recorded from our office."

"He did what?" Joe stuttered now alarmed? "He tapped our phones," Tony shot back, "please just read them." Joe sat there slumped back in his chair, his eyes staring out the window.

"What do they say Tony?" Joe quietly asked."

"I think you know."

"It's not what it seems Tony, I didn't have a choice."

"There's always a choice and you made a bad one," Tony quivered, no longer able to control his emotions. "You were my friend... how could you, HOW COULD YOU?" Holding his head in his hands, shaking up and down Joe blurted out,

"you let her die, Tom let her die. She was the best thing that happened to me and you let her die".... The room was silent as Joe tried to compose himself and continued, "I didn't mean for it to go this far; at first they told me they wanted to help get back at Black Rock for Lana's murder; they played me like a fiddle, told me I would have to give them something, just some information. Tony I never thought it would hurt anybody, you've got to believe me." Tony patiently listened to Joe's story, how Government operatives put the puzzle together from the bits and pieces of information Joe gave them. He knew first-hand how effective and coercive an experienced agency handler could be, and Joe was no match.

"I'm sorry for you," Tony said as Joe began to sob, "but you did a terrible thing and people died. I don't know what happens next but I can tell you one thing, I may forgive you but Tom won't."

A team of Federal investigators meticulously combed the launch site for a solid week, collecting and tagging evidence before activity at mission control resumed in earnest. The crew on Mars was considered stable now and Lazarus, at Tosky's insistence was being converted to handle the next scheduled mission, transporting a fully loaded cargo module, prioritizing the Martian build up. In addition to habitat dwellings needed for an expanding population the cargo log included over a thousand high efficiency thin film solar panels and mounting structures capable of generating 150,000 watts of electricity. Based on crew requests, a variety of freeze dried vegetables, meats and fruit were on board to supplement the additional prepackaged NASA type meals that over a sustained period of time became so unappetizing. Absent the heavy motorized equipment, originally transported by Horizon 1, sufficient capacity was available for a 1000 square foot prototype green house, complete with a climate control and hydration systems. Potting soils were included to mix with local Martian soils, to experiment with growing conditions. At my insistence a 2 man surgical team was integrated into the mission along with the medical supplies that would be needed to manage Jim Dougherty's condition. From the onset of the Horizon 1 mission, Alpha's flight control team began recording telemetry, creating a comprehensive profile of the ships performance. In the following weeks after the landing an extensive analysis revealed several design flaws and improvements that were needed; at the top of the list were additional redundancies to be built into the power panel controls and an independent auxiliary navigation computer capable of seamlessly taking over the operation of the ship at the flick of a switch. These and a dozen other modifications were in process now as the flight of Horizon 2 closed in on its launch date.

Listening to Bob Tosky relate the concessions the Administration had offered, Tony Colby couldn't believe what he was hearing. When he finished Colby's mouth remained open.

"This is a first Bob, never even heard of anything like this, you accepted it of course," Tony said questioningly.

"No, I told him I would think about it," Tosky replied in a dry tone of voice.

"THINK ABOUT IT, what the hell is there to think about? I can speak for Tom and I know he would jump all over it."

"I know, I know," Tosky shot back, "but we already have licensing commitments from some of the largest Aerospace companies on the planet and I have enough money to keep us going for a long time." Pacing back and forth now he added, "I'm not thrilled about Government involvement, the bureaucracy always complicates matters, slows things down and just when we're ready to explode." Colby paused for a moment collecting his thoughts.

"I know what you mean Bob, I really do, but you need to keep your ego in check, the US Government is bigger than us. We just went thru a very scary episode and I don't want to go thru something like that again."

"Relax Tony I'm not about to upset the applecart; they can have their Eminent Domain order - we still have the technology. Why the hell should we teach them how to put it together? Let them build their own fleet, by the time they get it right we'll be well on our way, besides I still don't trust the bastards. We're trying to play ball with the wrong team Tony, the real power is the Aerospace industry and together they have enough money to pull the strings on any administration." Tony began shaking his head,

"No, no Bob, that's a bad idea, we're either a part of this country or we're not, there's nothing in between. Those boys at justice gave their blood to help us and I gave my word, I won't be a part of this and neither will Tom." Tosky glared at Colby for an awkward moment, resenting the assertion.

"Don't misunderstand me Tony we're all in this together; I'm not trying to subvert the country, just want to make sure the Government stays off our backs."

Colby's words were still stinging Tosky's pride the next day and confirmation from D'Antonio left him feeling isolated, as he made the call to the Justice Department.

"Hello Brett, its Bob Tosky," pausing to carefully choose his words, "I've decided to accept your offer with a condition."

"Wait a minute Bob, there are no exceptions to this deal, its all or nothing."

"I won't accept the deal without it" Tosky adamantly replied."

"Damn it Tosky you're making this complicated," Allen consented in exasperation, "what's the condition?"

"I can refuse any proposed contract at any time without penalty or otherwise compromising the terms of the deal." The phones were silent for a moment as both men waited for the other to say something,

"I think I can sell that," Allen finally replied, "glad you're on board with this, I'll have the proposal sent over today." Walking out of his office Tosky began smiling, the sun was shining out of a clear blue sky and the door to Mars was wide open now. In the years to come mankind would pass thru to a new world and he was leading the way. A pioneering spirit welled up in him, thinking of the westward passage in America over a century before, only this time there would be no indigenous people to displace, only a new home for people to inhabit.

Launch day for Horizon 2 had arrived and except for the shape of the command module the rest of the ship had little resemblance to Horizon 1. In addition to the internal control and performance modifications installed, both the cargo and crew modules were reconfigured to a square shape. A spherical bullet configuration was originally adopted, simply as a matter of convention, what a space ship was supposed to look like; but as a result of slow near earth launch speed, the thinness of the Martian atmosphere and the emptiness of space, aerodynamic shapes served no redeeming purpose. Further refinements in navigation were made with the adoption of SOCAS, or "small object collision avoidance system." Telemetry from Horizon 1 had indicated that micro meteor detections were far enough out to allow for minor course adjustments, avoiding any possible collisions; once validated SOCAS was immediately adopted, since the necessary sensors were already in place requiring only a software modification to the flight control program. The ships design was quickly evolving adding performance and convenience features that could be added with known failure modes and redundant back ups; many other modifications called for would have to wait for further flight performance evaluations, while some were included on Horizon 2 as stand-alone simulated features. The ship was fully loaded now and contained a 6 man flight crew, 4 of whom would remain on Mars for at least one year. The return flight was scheduled for the remaining crew on Mars and the 2 man surgical team on Horizon 2, a total of 8, including myself, John Hodges, Jay Lanza, Phil Visi, Sue Lee and Lillian Banks while Jim Dougherty would remain to convalesce after surgery before returning home.

This time the scheduled launch of Horizon 2 seemed almost like a dry run. Aside from Alpha and ArmorTec personnel only a small group of NASA employees and tribal spectators were on hand for the unadvertised launch as the crew loaded into the ship. A grey morning sky seemed to envelope launch pad 1 in a shroud of secrecy except for the 2 additional ships now being assembled nearby. For the past month the construction of multiple launch pads were in the final stages of completion and the silhouette of the cargo modules for Horizon 3 and 4 loomed like sentinels standing guard. The Martian program was now in full stride, rapidly expanding under the growing demands of Government and commercial aerospace agencies for flight time and expeditionary trips to Mars. Horizon 2 silently lifted off on schedule and quickly pierced the low hanging clouds as the crowd cheered and waved knowing full well that the crew would have a bird's eye view of the spectators in the first few minutes of the flight. In short order mission control authorized high speed flight and Horizon 2 was on its way. Unlike the near disastrous flight of its predecessor the journey was uneventful and except for a few minor equipment glitches and course corrections the ship touched down at Oglala Station 5 days later.

The new square cargo module, now sitting adjacent to home base, appeared disproportionately smaller belying its greater volume and improvements in living space. Once unloaded the crews immediately began a planned construction effort initially supported by the Horizon 1 team. Utility hook ups for living quarters now doubled, provided regulated oxygen and electrical services and included a new interconnected sewage disposal system based on an accelerated putrefaction process. The system effectively rendered raw sewage and grey water an inert granular residue utilizing a flash vaporization process simplified by the thin Martian atmosphere. Initially powered by the nuclear generator, greater electrical output supplied by the new solar field once installed would greatly increase both efficiency and sewage processing rates. Located less than 100 yards outside of the Oglala compound a full acre of aluminum mounting structure rose up in precise rows supporting new high performance solar panels. Recent breakthroughs in panel design based on multiple silicon wafers were able to capture electrical output over a broader light spectrum essentially doubling the efficiency of a standard panel. Once installed the panels performed flawlessly capable of functioning as the primary electrical utility for the entire station or as a parallel redundant service. Either way Oglala station now had ample electrical capacity to support current and future requirements for an expanding base. The green house although quickly erected required continuous adjustments to maintain the desired temperature and moisture control suitable for earth based growing conditions. Given the extreme Martian temperature fluctuations it soon became evident that significant equipment and control system modifications or more tolerant plant varieties would be required; the initial green-house design was more a proof of concept rather than a prototype but capable of providing extensive operational data to support the development of a true prototype. Early on however, an unknown seed strain accidentally mixed with a blend of virgin Martian and Earth soils and remained hidden until small green leafs broke thru the soil sprouting an extensive subsurface root system. The plant appeared hardy and grew rapidly, where other seeds either completely failed or barely grew. A thorough chemical analysis confirmed the plant origin was unknown and quite possibly a new species somehow spawned by a combination of Martian climate, soils and gravity, in short a mutation. Its most significant feature however was its composition, consisting of protein, carbohydrates and fatty acids, a complete food staple. The new plant, dubbed Martian Maze, was unexpected and possibly simply an anomaly but like the proverbial mustard seed it had the power to develop a truly autonomous civilization.

These were the primary activities conducted during the first weeks by the new Martian team. Guided by myself and the Horizon 1 crew the initial workload and transition to the station routine dictated by the Martian environment was quickly adopted and now the first return flight, the second leg of the rescue mission was at hand. John Hodges and Jay Lanza were occupied confirming pre-launch check lists with mission control, while Phil Visi and I loaded provisions and equipment slated for repair or decommissioning. Other than personal effects, selected Martian rock and soil specimens would be the last artifacts to be stowed aboard ship just prior to launch. Now 24 hours from lift off the Launch clock was set at 2PM Martian time to allow for an afternoon touchdown 6 days later at our South Dakota facility. Sitting in the conference center of home base any team business discussed was never a private matter; the only seclusion available was restricted to each member's private quarters and that too was limited at best. Staring out at the Martian landscape while pondering the trip home Sue Lee interrupted my thoughts,

"Tom we need to talk, do you have a few minutes?"

"Oh, hi Sue," I lazily replied, waking out of my daydream "sure, what's up?"

"I'm staying here with Jim," she tersely announced; not sure I heard her correctly and with a confused look on my face asked,

"You're staying where?"

"Tom listen to me," she firmly demanded, "I'm not going back, I won't leave Jim in this condition." As she continued Lillian Banks and Jay Lanza walked up behind her noticeably holding hands, before I could say anything, Lillian added in a resolute tone of voice

"We're staying too." Now fully awake and somewhat alarmed at these demands, I began while standing up,

"You do realize I'm still in charge here and the protocol to do something is a request, not an ultimatum. In short my reply is out of the question, DO YOU UNDERSTAND - out of the question." Sue Lee began shaking her head,

"No Tom, we've earned the right to make this decision, besides you can't stop us if we won't go."

"Look here Sue," I replied in an agitated voice, "I can't lock you up since we don't have a jail on Mars yet…. but make no mistake I won't allow anything to jeopardize the program and if that means physically putting you aboard ship and tying you down, I'll damn well do that."

"Easy Tom, nobody is threatening the mission," Jay Lanza calmly cut in. "If any of us thought that we'd be the first to admit it and I think you know that."

"Yea and how's that?" I skeptically replied, getting hold of my anger.

"Think about it Tom," Jay continued, "the station needs a full time physician and Jim's still not out of the woods yet, we'll also need an experienced communications expert to maintain the link with mission control, and who's going to maintain systems we don't even have schematics for? The new crew is barely able to handle a fully functioning one, nothing like what we managed to patch together from the command module wreckage. No, we're not threatening the mission Tom we're helping it." After Jay finished I remained quiet for a while, his point made sense but breaking a command structure in this way was a bad precedent to set, something I could not allow or at least had an obligation to remedy.

"I'll let you know my decision at our pre-flight meeting later today," I said walking away, "in the mean time I'll expect you to comply with my decision and be ready to depart." Not waiting for a reply I promptly left. Sue was right I really had no way of forcing a crew member to return and I wasn't about to capture and tie her down, but my first obligation was to maintain discipline and a command structure.

A steady stream of aerospace executives had inundated Alpha headquarters since bids for DREAM licenses were advertised a week ago. With concurrence from D'Antonio, Tosky wasted no time soliciting all of the brand name companies in the aerospace consortiums of the US and European Union. Initially 5 licenses were being offered requiring a 5 billion dollar cash deposit which would immediately revert to an initial licensing fee upon acceptance of a proposal. In addition a sliding scale royalty was imposed ranging from 5 to 10% based on gross revenues with minimum annuals set at the 1 billion dollar mark. These and other limitations including a renewable 10 year licensing term, stringent purchasing and use restrictions and technology improvement rights were hard deals, maybe too hard but nevertheless DREAM was the only deal in town at least for the time being. Tosky also knew that once the Government got involved despite the best of intentions, technology leaks would inevitably spawn independent and unauthorized operators, many outside the legal system of the west. Now was the time to capture the big players in the Industry, particularly since the US Government had already started converting an old shuttle launch pad at the Kennedy Space Center to handle DREAM vehicles. Of course Industry players we're also well aware of this dynamic but their own greed would not allow them to fall behind any potential competitor and Tosky was betting on that; he was masterful at this game and ruthlessly played it for all its worth. Tony Colby began skeptically listening to Tosky's conversation over his intercom with the President of Atlas Rocket; Tosky patiently sat there as the Atlas chief ran on about the benefits of working with his company and the money he was about to plunk down on behalf of DREAM. In the Shuttle days Arthur Daily was referred to as the "blue plate special" a related insider at Atlas he was groomed for the top slot early on and everyone knew it. Any indiscretion or bump in the road had always been overlooked but this was different, any mistake here could be catastrophic, met with immediate termination. There just was no room to hide from this or blame others.

"Bob I hope you realize this deal could make or break Atlas," Daily urgently said, "I've got my ass on the line here and I need to know you'll guarantee that we'll get this done." Tosky looked over at Tony and winked.

"Arthur, DREAM is not a new concept it's a proven technology going thru a 2nd generation upgrade, what the hell are you worried about? If your company is as good as you say it is you won't have a problem, besides, what guarantee could I give you? We have no control over outer space; once you leave the planet you're on your own….. Listen Arthur I've got several company reps banging on my door right now, you have the solicitation, you either believe in DREAM or you don't. When I see a check on my desk, I'll know you're in; otherwise I wish you well in your endeavors." Tosky not waiting for a response hung up the phone, as Tony Colby began to laugh out loud.

The launch clock for the return flight of Horizon 2 read 4 hours and 12 minutes, barely enough time to finish a final systems check and button down the crew for lift off. Anticipation started to build as the crew gathered for the launch briefing at home base.

"Alright let's get back into flight mode," I hollered over the intercom; "we've got a busy schedule to work before we leave. You all have a copy of your scheduled mission assignments, but as of now it's changed. Sue, Lillian and Jay have asked to stay on to assure the safety and operation of home base in our absence and I believe that's in the best interest of the mission and all concerned. We'll re-man a flight schedule once we're on our way and in the meantime please pack your gear aboard ship and suit up for lift off." Everyone appeared startled and began looking around at each other; they knew why Sue wanted to stay but were caught by surprise by Lillian and Jay. Lillian was stoic in her replies as to why....

"first of all someone has to keep the mission going and Jay and I are a team," Lillian said in a matter of fact tone, "and you don't think I'm going to let Sue stay here by herself and go thru the ordeal of a pregnancy alone." Accidentally letting Sue Lee's secret out Lillian hesitated and began to blush, looking over at Sue embarrassingly. Sue Lee rolled her eyes and groaned.

"It's OK everyone may as well know now; besides I always wanted to be the first family somewhere, even if not on earth." A nervous laughter echoed in the room and quickly died out, another unexpected complication I thought but not enough time to do anything about it. We were finally going home and nothing, absolutely nothing was going to screw that up.

Time quickly passed and the return flight of Horizon 2 was on its way. This time there was no sense of discovery, no excitement other than normal flight jitters and a familiar routine of managing the journey home although if all went well the flight would be autonomously handled by the Nav computer. Still there were several days of tedium in front of us, watching the ships metrics at the control console and the picture like emptiness of space. It had been a long journey, since we first left earth and I was anxious to return home again, good old mother earth, blue skies and green grass and I thought some female TLC would go a long way to prop up my sagging morale. Curiously as the Martian silhouette began to shrink in the distance I also felt a sense of loss, of leaving home again and wondering when or if I would return. The trip was thankfully uneventful, DREAM and the NAV computer performed flawlessly touching down in South Dakota precisely as scheduled – 3PM on the 15th of May 2020. A small group of medical and support staff from mission control greeted us as we exited the ship. After a short congratulatory welcome home we were ferried away to a nearby apartment like medical hold over facility for a few days of physical examination and mission debriefing. Although physically drained from the constant pressure of managing crew affairs and my own emotional turmoil over Mars, the R & R was therapeutic; only in retrospect did I begin to realize how debilitated I had gotten possibly jeopardizing the lives of the crew and the future of the program. We were lucky this time, I thought, and desperately needed a more experienced player on our team and that meant getting NASA involved and its play book of lessons learned over the past 60 years.

Pondering these issues while walking into the cafeteria I couldn't help overhearing Phil Visi arguing with our 1st officer,

"John I'm not crazy I've been looking at this stuff for over a month now." Phil was becoming loud and animated as I interrupted,

"Hey fellows can I play to?"

"Oh hi Tom," John Hodges said, "sure, sit down and listen to Phil's new rendition of Einstein's general theory of relativity." Phil groaned a forced laugh and went on.

"This is not bullshit I've been looking at our telemetry for the past month and I tell you our flight navigation calculations are slightly off."

"So what are you saying Phil, our whole concept of space-time is wrong?"

"That's not what I'm saying, at least not yet, but those little navigation anomalies we saw in flight were not just random events or minor equipment glitches, they followed a consistent pattern."

"Now that's crazy Phil," I replied, "there has to be a logical explanation for this, you must have missed something."

"Maybe Tom, but if I'm right this is unprecedented, and I'm betting it has something to do with dark energy."

Waking up in my condo seemed surreal, I dreamt of it many times over the past few months and at the moment of waking it took a few seconds to distinguish dreams from reality. I had been sleeping in late for the past week and was ready, even energized to get back into the game. The familiar site of ArmorTec's offices put a smile on my face as I walked into the lobby. Marie saw me first, running into my arms; hugging her female form seemed almost erotic as we pressed our cheeks together.

"Where have you been handsome?" she said pulling me by the arm. "Come with me there's somebody waiting to see you in the conference room." Turning into the doorway cheers erupted from the crowd packed into the conference room; "WELCOME HOME" our whole staff shouted shaking my hand and slapping my back – the outpouring caught me by surprise as emotions unexpectedly welled up in my chest while my voice quivered thanking everyone in the room. In short order music began to play from somewhere in the lobby as a team of caterer's started setting up, a full blown party was quickly getting into gear as more familiar faces began emerging. Tony Colby bear hugged me as Bob Tosky laughed rubbing my head.

"In case you don't know it, you're a wealthy man now Tom," Tosky said, "how does that make you feel?"

"It's always good to have a few extra bucks lying around" I casually replied, "but it doesn't surprise me I had good teammates backing me up."

"SURPRISE YOU, SURPRISE YOU," Tony jokingly hollered, "you're not just wealthy you arrogant bastard, you're a billionaire now, and that's no bullshit the money's in the bank. As it turned out Colby was only partially right I now had a bank account with over 6 billion in it and growing daily. Over the next few days I got caught up with DREAM business details both commercially and inside the Government. Tosky did a remarkable job, he wasn't taking any prisoners and pressed DREAMs advantage to the brink. Sitting in Tosky's office at Alpha headquarters I had just finished reviewing the last of 5 completed licensing agreements. Shaking my head in amazement I said

"No one would believe this could have happened so fast Bob, it's just incredible."

"That's because DREAM is incredible Tom, I only took advantage of what you put in place."

"You make it sound so simple," I replied in an incredulous tone of voice, "you literally created what may turn out to be another industrial revolution overnight; where do you think we go from here?"

"Same as before Tom, I think we focus on the transportation industry, make that our own, put our stamp on it and let the Aerospace moguls fight over the rest of the industrial space."

"I wish I had your vision Bob, this is way over my head. Besides I'm still too focused on the Mars program right now to think about anything else." Tosky laughed and waved his hand,

"Don't worry partner that'll pass and in the meantime I've got your back."

Rocket-dyne, a new wholly owned subsidiary of DREAM Industries was now operating 24/7 trying to keep up with licensing orders for DREAM engines. At the same time mission control in South Dakota, in addition to handling the Horizon series ship assembly operations continued to manage astronaut recruitment and training assisted by an on-site NASA team. Program growth normally evolving over years was taking place in a matter of months. This fast track expansion, fueled by an excess of program funding, paralleled the DREAM conversion of Government Launch facilities at Cape Canaveral Florida and Houston Texas. In the middle of this whirlwind of activity a dual mission was being readied for the first night time launch. Horizon 3 and 4 would lift off 4 hours apart bringing a full complement of technical and scientific personnel, a wide range of equipment and provisions and enough light weight titanium structure for the first stage construction of a planned geodesic dome spanning over 4 acres atop Oglala station.

Martian Greenhouse

The Dome canopy would enclose 10 converted Cargo modules, laid out in a circular orientation, consisting of a hospital unit, a mission control up-link station, an upscale hotel module for visiting personnel and transportation customers and 7 self-contained housing modules. In the center a small town like courtyard was designed for entertainment, recreation, and exercise activities and once sealed and aerated would provide an earth like unfettered environment accommodating at least 100 people. On the out skirts of the dome, landing and launch pads are located stationing the return craft modules, a newly installed solar field and a nearby area suitable for a large green house providing a sustainable food supply for the Station. Interconnecting these and future support facilities a series of single lane gravel roads were planned for quickly hauling personnel and materials in and about Oglala Station. In 24 hours with the launch of Horizon 3 and 4, plans for the expansion of the first Martian community would begin to quickly become a reality. The logistics and coordination needed to accomplish all of this was staggering, not to mention the frightening outflow of money; enough infrastructure was being readied for the coming invasion, a Martian invasion and zero hour was here.

Chapter 10

ENGINEERING A PLANET

Rapid City airport was starting to feel like home as my connecting flight out of Minneapolis rolled into its docking gate. Not the easiest city to get to but it was a refreshing contrast to the crowded, mechanical atmosphere of the larger airport Hubs. People smiled and somehow you never had to run to catch a flight; and intuitively I knew I would miss the casual pace here, when DREAM Industry's primary space based operations would shift over to Cape Canaveral. The decision to relocate was an easy one for financial reasons but the emotional baggage of the Sioux and start-up operations there had become a part of me and would be hard to let go. In any event we were at least 6 months away from making the move and the South Dakota facility would still be retained as a secondary space port, especially desirable for any activities space based or otherwise preferably kept out of the media and secure from the prying eyes of any potential Aerospace competitor. Walking into mission control, I arrived as Horizon 3 was lifting off – the control room was deceptively calm as check list and performance chatter was casually being exchanged between the Horizon 3 crew and flight techs. You could always find the Flight Director after a successful launch by looking for a plume of cigar smoke – although in a smoke free facility this indiscretion, an Apollo Program carryover, was ignored,

"Hey Bill, these launches are starting to look like a walk in the park," I jokingly said; "pretty casual if you ask me." Bill Heaney was a friend and a mentor and my first flight training instructor; recognizing my voice he never looked up and kept staring at his monitor as he cracked a smile.

"In the first place nobody asked you rooky and how the hell would you know?" he growled, standing up and added shaking my hand, "You never could tell the difference. Sure good to see you again Tom, what brings you back here? I thought all this work and sweat stuff was beneath you."

"Well you know, can't teach an old dog new tricks; I'm hooked like you Bill, it's in my blood. Have you seen Visi lately?"

"Not lately Tom, he's been holed up in the lab for the past few days; keeps on sending in requests for flight telemetry details. What's that all about?"

"Maybe nothing but you know Phil, if something doesn't look right he won't stop till he finds out why."

It was getting dark by the time I got to the lab, a dim light shown in the back of the room reflecting the shadow of a body hunched over a desk.

"Phil Visi," I hollered entering the building.

"I'm back here," came the reply.

"Oh good you're not dead," I said reaching his desk, "but you look like shit buddy, this is not the way a billionaire is supposed to look."

"Yea I heard Tom, but this is driving me nuts."

"Don't tell me you're still analyzing the course adjustments?" I asked incredulously, "the so called anomalies?"

"One and the same Tom – look, when you first asked me to get involved I told you what you found could be very important, which it is but I meant very important to me. The team worked out the engineering and we went to Mars, and that's great, but we never looked at the science, not really and that's my bailiwick; it's what gets me up in the morning; it's why I went to Mars. Can you understand that?" Surprised at Phil's intensity I hesitated;

"I do Phil, you know I've always believed we were put here, not just for a reason but for a special reason and we waste most of our lives avoiding it. You don't know it yet but you're a lucky man you found it."

"Thanks Tom, I needed that. People around here are starting to think I've gone loco, they even have a name for it, MARTIAN DISTROPHY."

"While we're at it, why don't you show me what you've got so far- maybe I can help." Phil began pulling marked charts out of a ruffled collection of telemetry data; "see here, the course adjustments going to and from Mars are perfect mirror images. They occurred at the same time and the same degree; now that's not a random event." I nodded agreement. "So I recomputed the trajectory calculations for Horizon 2's return flight based on earlier course correction data and presto, I came up with an adjusted flight path that wouldn't require a course correction - that's significant."

"I'll say it is, what else have you got?"

"Only speculation at this point Tom; as you know the motion of celestial bodies conform to Einstein's general theory of relativity and reams of orbital data have always confirmed the validity of celestial calculations and in particular computations for manned and unmanned missions. However these objects are traveling at relatively slow speeds, less than 100,000 MPH. DREAM vehicles are traveling an order of magnitude faster and it seems the course corrections only occur at speeds in excess of 500,000 MPH. The only two things that make us different are speed and DREAM and somehow, I believe that's where we'll find the answer."

The thought that Einstein might have been mistaken or at least inaccurate was almost inconceivable given the scrutiny of a world-wide scientific body over the past 100 years; and even if Phil's speculation was off base his flight path data was irrefutable. I was spending another restless night after returning home from South Dakota wrestling with Phil's observations, until the annoying sound of a ringing phone broke into my consciousness,

"Tom, are you there? It's Tony".........

"Tony.. Tony Colby?" I asked in a confused tone of voice; "what the hell time is it?"

"Wake up, put your feet on the floor and get dressed." Colby demanded, "Bob Tosky is being held at gunpoint in his office and it appears you're the only one that can save his ass."

"WOA, me… WHY ME?" I yelled in surprise.

"Just get over here Tom before things spin out of control. The bastard holding the gun wants you here within the hour or he's gonna start shooting." Alpha headquarters was normally a 30 minute drive from my condo, but a high speed, late morning race got me there 15 minutes later. The lobby now cordoned off with cops stopped anyone approaching within 20 feet of the building – finally Tony Colby spotted me behind a barricade and sent an officer to escort me to a command room set up by the FBI.

"Who the hell is this guy Tony?" I asked out of breath, from behind me, a gravelly voice interrupted,

"is this D'Antonio Mr. Colby?" Tony nodded, "I'm agent Brewer Mr. D'Antonio," he said shaking my hand, "Mr. Tosky is being held by an armed abductor in an office 50 feet from here. Things are stable for the time being but it's a very delicate situation, he's threatened to kill Mr. Tosky unless you agree to certain contract stipulations regarding your space program."

"OK, OK I'll agree," I skeptically replied.

"I'm afraid it's not that easy Mr. D'Antonio."

"Yea I had a feeling it wouldn't be; by the way my real name is Tom - why don't you call me that." Brewer didn't appreciate the humor.

"Mr. D'Antonio this is not a game," he replied in a cynical tone of voice; "a man's life is at stake!" Tired and worried the blood flushed my face reacting to the sarcasm

"THAT'S MY PARTNER IN THERE," I hollered, aggressively pointing my finger in his face. "Don't lecture me; I know damn well how serious this is." Surprised at the outburst Agent Brewer shoved my hand aside as Tony Colby stepped in between us.

"This is not going down this way" he firmly demanded; "if you two can't work together we're going to lose Tosky."

Turning away at the remark while getting hold of my emotions I said,

"Alright Brewer, what do you need me to do?" Backing away Brewer nodded at Tony and looked directly at me -

"nothing right now Tom; we have a negotiator on an office line talking with him. By the way" he calmly added, "my name is Gary."

Another hour of negotiations amounted to nothing, only more threats on Tosky's life. The abductor turned out to be the Atlas Rocket exec Tosky played hard ball with, Arthur Daily, aka "The Blue Plate Special." Incensed at the terms of the DREAM licensing agreement Daily accepted, the Atlas board gave him an ultimatum; GET A BETTER DEAL OR RESIGN. The thought of losing Atlas was too much and Daily was prepared to do whatever it took to get that deal even murder. He was becoming more erratic and delusional by the hour despite repeated calls and assurances from family and Atlas management and it was now obvious that talking him out was no longer an option; a rescue attempt would be needed. The morning quickly passed into evening as our negotiator was becoming hard pressed to maintain a line of communication distracting Daily from the violence he swore. Tosky's office had a large window behind his desk with an unobstructed view of the buildings across the street. Early on agents were deployed there to maintain visual access inside the office, now being broadcast to a terminal at our command post. In addition several sharp shooters were positioned at adjoining buildings with a clear view of the window behind Tosky's desk. However the view exposed only part of the office, and whether intentional or not, Daily was holding Tosky in the unexposed part. The marksmen now had orders to take Daily down if a clean shot became available, preferably a head shot, to eliminate any possible return fire. On the other side in front of our command post two agents with automatic weapons were stationed along the partition covering the unexposed part of Tosky's office. If Tosky could be separated from Daily and somehow move to the exposed area, the blind area supposedly holding only Daily would be strafed with automatic weapons fire thru the partition while, at the same time, heavily armored agents would break thru the office door setting off flash/bang munitions disorienting and immobilizing any occupant still standing.

This was the plan and my role was to come up with a way to lure Tosky by himself into the exposed area.

"Arthur it's Tom D'Antonio," I called over the office line, "are you there?" ......after a brief pause a shaky voice replied,

"I'm here."

"I know what you want Arthur and I've got it right here."

"Don't insult me Tom," Daily answered, "I know there's no good way out of this, I'm not stupid."

"Yes there is Arthur. We both know you have to give yourself up, but I have a signed legal document here that gives you the terms you wanted and we're doing it because we need Atlas technology to move ahead; we couldn't do it without you and you've made us realize that." Again silence for what seemed like an hour –

"Yea well I knew that all along. I told Tosky he needed us, we would have made a great team, but no, you arrogant ass (now addressing Tosky) you had to rub my face it, make me beg - well how do you like it now? I'm holding all the cards." Fearful at his emotional outburst I started yelling into the phone,

"ARTHUR, **ARTHUR**…. if we're going to get out of this I need you to concentrate; listen to me, you may have to pay for this even do a little jail time but I'll testify for you; you'll get away with a slap on the wrist,".…..more silence and the sound of sobbing.

"Tom I always thought you were a fair man," again sobbing, "but I'm a standup guy too… that's why I'm here; do you think this was easy for me?"

"Of course not Arthur, I know that but now we have to move on and end this."

"I know the FBI routine Tom. Those guys will blow my head off the second I walk out the door."

"Not if you do as I say Arthur, no one will shoot you."

"You're wrong Tom, they will shoot me,"

"Not if I walk out with you,".…..

"I'm listening" Daily replied.

"Walk over to the door, let me in and let Tosky go, then hand me your gun so no one has any reason to shoot and we'll walk out together."

"That's real cute Tom, I told you before I'm not stupid; the minute I show myself in front of the window the snipers across the street will blow me away." Daily's awareness of the circumstances caught all of us by surprise. Agent Brewer put his hand over the phone and whispered,

"Tell him to send Tosky to let you in so he doesn't have to expose himself. We'll get a clean shot at him thru the partition."

"No, no it's too risky Gary, I think I can talk him out." Brewer impatiently threw his hands up and looked over at Colby,

"Yes you might," Tony interrupted, "and then again you might not. They're the experts Tom, you should do it their way. Tony was right this wasn't my bag but nevertheless the thought of walking another human being into a death trap was disconcerting regardless of the circumstances. On the other hand Bob Tosky's life hung in the balance and that was enough for me. Arthur Daily believed he had one and only one chance to redeem himself at Atlas and to walk out of this alive.

"Tosky take off your coat and glasses," Daily demanded, "and sit on the floor over here."

"Wait a minute, what the hell are you taking about?" Tosky protested in an alarmed tone of voice….. "I heard D'Antonio he wants me to walk out."

"Shut your mouth and do what I say," Daily hissed, "I have a different plan and you're going to be my ticket out of here."

Barely 2 weeks had passed since the departure of Horizon 2 and with the arrival of Horizon 3 and 4 the Martian program was taking a major leap forward. Despite the on-going hostage drama on Earth, nothing could or would stop this momentum with so many pieces and organizations in motion. The Martian population now boasted a complement of 22 technical, medical and engineering personnel all highly motivated and dedicated to the creation of a Martian community. However these intrepid travelers would soon conform to the pragmatic restrictions and work conditions imposed by the Martian environment. First encountered by their predecessors, the lessons learned, based on the activity log of Horizon 1 were invaluable to any new Martian arrival. Although a thousand and one lesser projects needed attention dome construction had top priority and held everyone's highest expectations. To expedite construction an advanced project engineering group at Alpha, with the assistance of NASA developed a small flying lift vehicle dubbed "Sky Crane" (based on a decade-old NASA design used in the unmanned Curiosity program); a 2-man vehicle powered by new, higher density DREAM panels capable of lifting and precisely positioning the structural components of the Geodesic Dome. In addition, although quite small, the Sky Crane could easily capture and lift a wide range of materials and sub-assemblies, even cargo modules if required.

Curiosity's Sky Crane

Since the on-set of ice pack drilling operations, several million gallons of water had been recovered, and consumed, broken down into its components or simply evaporated into the thin Martian atmosphere. Measurements taken in and around Oglala Station had recently recorded a slight change in atmospheric pressure and although barely readable, it was the first evidence of terraforming activity. Accelerating this activity a million times faster would provide the impetus for transforming Mars from a red to a blue planet, capable of supporting human habitation. The possibilities were endless but would have to await future generations and yet the thought was still thrilling; to be part of it made the entire community part of something larger, a feeling of ownership and the desire to make a home more livable.

Second generation green-house controls were included in the equipment log of Horizon 4 and once refitted into the prototype unit quickly improved growing conditions almost overnight, evident in the reinvigorated plant life struggling to break into the daylight. Ever since the discovery of Martian Maze, botanical experiments attempting to improve this potential food source, yielded another mutation; a sterile flower like sprig capable of spreading without any fruit or seed bearing growth. This amazing plant would now yield another potential life changing feature – GRASS, and if capable of further adaptations, a rapid terraforming mechanism would be found.

At the present time there are 4 cargo modules located at the station; the Horizon 1 module now used as a mission control and temporary hospital unit and 2, 3 and 4 modules as permanent living quarters. To complete the planned expansion another 6 modules were needed; 2 of which, Horizon 5 and 6 were being fitted out at the Sioux facility in S. Dakota and the remaining 4 would shortly be underway as soon as rehabbing operations concluded at our Cape Canaveral facility. Although all 10 of the modules would be contained under the Station Dome, much of the preliminary construction work was scheduled for completion prior to their arrival. Surveying operations for the Dome perimeter already underway would be immediately followed by the construction of a concrete foundation. Using a specially formulated concrete blend for rapidly changing temperature extremes, a combination of chemical additives in addition to a heated tent structure covering the days pour would be needed for curing purposes. These and many other custom details adopted in a labor intensive process kept slowing things down despite our best efforts and the use of heavy equipment. On the other hand once complete, preassembled subsections of the dome could be quickly positioned and secured in place, compliments of the Sky Crane.

All of these activities were preplanned and meticulously documented, and orchestrating the right balance of labor, material and equipment was essential to maintain budgets. But delays and changes were becoming the norm. We were still on the wrong side of a major learning curve and screw ups were escalating with an ever increasing range of activities. Management oversight, 60 million miles away, required something more than business as usual and NASA's expertise was again called upon. In short order the elaborate work procedures and instruction booklets provided with each project were relegated to the status of a project guide and all work activities would now be driven by autonomous project teams. Meeting daily assessing work progress and issues, a hands-on management format affording practical solutions quickly began eating into a growing work backlog. Unlike the first close knit inhabitants of Oglala Station, the new Martian community was becoming more diverse and independent and the next step in its evolution was the formation of a governing body. Up till now a centralized military like structure provided the organization and discipline guiding the initial phases of the program and now having served its purpose would soon be replaced by a business model.

Only silence hung in the air outside Bob Tosky's office for what seemed like an eternity, along with 2 Federal agents with full body armor and a bag of specialized munitions designed to disorient and stun anyone within 20 feet of their detonation. Now ready with a door banger sledge hammer, to literally knock a door off its hinges, the rescue team nervously awaited the go ahead from Agent Brewer.

"Arthur I'm waiting," my voice echoed in the hall; "open the door and we all go home."

"OK, OK I hear you Tom," came a muffled reply then briefly after what sounded like a scuffle…Daily added, "I'm sending Tosky over to open the door." Everyone now on high alert watched a man's figure walk into the windowed space of the office towards the door.

"It's Tosky" Brewer whispered, signaling the agents in the hall…on the count of 3 to simultaneously strafe the office partition exposed in the hall while knocking in the office door and setting off flash bang and smoke munitions. Raising his hand and watching the video link inside the office, his first, second and third fingers were raised in quick succession, setting loose the deafening sound of automatic weapons fire and explosions inside the office. Seconds later, as smoke filled the halls outside the office a team member half carried and pushed Tosky out the door into an adjoining hall while the Agent inside hollered

"Suspect down, all clear." Rushing in along with an EMT team we quickly located a limp body laying face down on the floor. Walking over to the body I felt squeamish expecting to see Arthur Daily's bullet riddled body as Agent Brewer rolled his torso over. Hesitating, peering at his face thru the smoke the shock and panic hit me,

"Its Bob Tosky," I hollered in disbelief, kneeling down holding Tosky's shoulder. "Bob, it's Tom, can you hear me?" I asked in desperation. "Bob answer me," I insisted now shaking both his shoulders, suddenly he moaned and opened his eyes, as the EMTs stabilized his body moving him onto a gurney.

"Tom… is that you, what the hell happened? Did I make it…. did they shoot the bastard?"

Agent Brewer knew immediately what happened. Once again Daily's grasp of the situation was underestimated; as soon as Brewer saw Tosky laying on the floor he charged out into the hallway where moments before Daily was being ferreted out to safety. The hall now empty led to a fire stairway and an exit one floor down.

"We can stop now Mr. Tosky," the rescue officer said, grabbing Daily by his arm, "it's all clear." Swiveling around while pulling a pistol out from inside his jacket, Daily blankly looked directly at the officer and fired a single shot into his belly. Brewer opened the exit door just in time to see the officer slump down falling to the ground.

"Take one more step you miserable son of a bitch, and I'll blow your goddamn head off." Daily flinched at the unexpected voice, then ducked and bolted around a corner as Agent Brewer fired a shot and missed. By this time several other agents coming out of the front of the building cordoned off the area – Daily was now trapped hiding behind a Dumpster in an alleyway used for the building's trash removal.

"Give it up Daily, there's no way out," Agent Brewer's voice rang out; "this is your last chance."

"Let me talk with D'Antonio."

"You shot a cop," Brewer adamantly answered, "there won't be any negotiation."

"I'm here Arthur," I called out.

"Tom, I didn't mean to shoot anybody; you've got to make them understand that - it just happened."

"Doesn't matter now Arthur; If you give yourself up no one else needs to get hurt."

"I can't Tom, I can't… I'll never survive in a jail cell." Somehow I felt sorry for Daily; like me he spent most of his adult life trying to run a business and doing the right thing. I knew Tosky pushed him hard… maybe too hard and the man broke and I was partly responsible for conning him into this mess. Without thinking I jumped out into the open and started walking toward Daily holding my hand up to Brewer to wait.

"Arthur I'm unarmed, come on out and I'll do what I can to help you."

"Alright Tom, alright," he replied walking out from behind the dumpster.

"Give me your gun Arthur," I said as we approached each other. Suddenly Daily stopped,

"My gun, MY GUN?" he asked, with a strange look on his face, it's the only thing I've got left Tom, you know I can't do that."

"Arthur don't do this," I pleaded becoming more concerned, "I'll protect you - just give me the gun." Daily grinned looking at me,

"You know Tom we would have made a great team together."

"We still can Arthur, we still can."

"Yes we can Tom," he calmly agreed, "but not in this life." With that Arthur Daily, aka the Blue Plate Special placed the muzzle of his gun securely under his chin and without hesitating pulled the trigger.

Reminiscing the activities of the past month, watching clouds roll by thru my office window, Marie's voice interrupted my day dreaming.

"Tom, you've got a visitor;" suspicious at the lack of her usual visitor details I walked into the lobby and froze in surprise.

"Hello Tom it's been awhile," Joe Campo greeted me in a somber tone of voice. "I wanted to let you know first-hand my side of the story….figured at least I owed you that." For an awkward moment a tense silence filled the air.

"Ok Joe," I tersely replied and motioned him into my office. Closing the door I looked at him questioningly. "You don't have to do this; I know you had your reasons"….

"I have to Tom," he replied, avoiding eye contact, "the guilt is killing me. I'm not looking for forgiveness or pity, I don't deserve that."

"What the hell do you want?" I impatiently interrupted; "did you think we would just shake hands as if nothing happened?" Now getting animated and raising my voice, "people died Joe, you almost got me and the entire crew killed." Pacing the floor, my outburst contorting his face in pain,

"I know that Tom, I think about it every day, when I wake up and go to bed it's always there and I can't take it back, or make it right. I tell you it's crushing me." Getting up to leave Joe waved his hand in resignation, "just wanted to tell you how I felt Tom, I didn't mean to upset you." Watching Joe it was clear he had reached rock bottom and had no place else to go. A long time ago I hit bottom after a degrading divorce and couldn't help remembering how a chance meeting with him helped me snap out of it.

"Wait a minute Joe, maybe I can help…… tell me what you really want;" turning around, his face flushed, he replied

"Redemption Tom, Redemption… I've got to find a way to earn it somehow."

Bob Tosky walked out of the hospital after a 3 week stay. Originally admitted in critical condition, the gun-shot wounds to his legs turned out to be flesh wounds inflicting some nerve damage; he could walk but it would now be with a permanent limp. Although he would have to convalesce for another month a virtual office was set up in his home to monitor the activities at Alpha headquarters. Since his and my absence the Mars program never missed a beat. Long term plans were in place and a competent management staff independently ran the program, even the Governments plans were ahead of schedule and our Cape Canaveral facility was now operational.

"Good morning Tom, it's Bob."

"Well you sound better," I replied, "how the hell do you feel?"

"Never better, in fact too good I'm getting bored." "Uh Oh, now you're scaring me, the last time I heard that we started a war."

"Tom I want a seat on the next Mars flight."

"Hold on Tiger, you'd have to bump a scheduled crew slot, and you know damn well you'll never pass medical now."

"Well we'll just have to make an exception!"

"Can't do that Bob, our insurances won't allow it and I refuse to jeopardize a mission." The phone was silent for a long moment and I could sense Tosky beginning to fume on the other end.

"Don't give me that bullshit Tom I don't care who I have to bump I'm going and that's final."

"Calm down buddy, you can't go in a crew slot, I won't allow it and neither will our safety protocols that we all signed off on, but you can go as a guest." Again silence and a brief pause,

"What do you mean?"

"We can get you a ticket on any flight, we're going weekly now, but you'll strictly be a visitor and you'll have to wait until the hotel module is up and running."

Martian activity was now going on 24/7 and its population was increasing monthly. The autonomous field teams instituted by NASA operated on independent schedules so that the station never slept or shut down. Oglala Station was now incorporated as a foreign American city, administered by a private commercial enterprise, "Oglala City LLC" - OC, a wholly owned subsidiary of DREAM Enterprises, was managed by a joint venture between Alpha, ArmorTec, and NASA. The first administrator chosen for OC was the prior Chief Operating Officer for Apple; the selection indicative of the role that advanced sensors, communications and the many faces of information technology would play in this alien environment. No longer exclusively considered an exploratory scientific mission the next phase of the Martian enterprise was at hand; to develop an exciting atmosphere attracting billions in investments and a rush of humanity to take a bite out of this new apple. OC would be repackaged and branded as the new out-of-this-world resort, including tax free employment opportunities and semi-permanent residences. Over the next few months the Dome over the city was completed ahead of schedule, thanks in large measure to the agile capabilities of the Sky Crane.

Until a sustainable food supply could be harvested and relied on from an expanded green house facility, commissary activities were hectic trying to keep up with feeding the ever growing volume of field teams. A wide variety of provisions were constantly being ferried in and stored in large refrigeration units located just outside the dome; although provisions normally considered perishable on Earth, remained dormant in the thin Martian atmosphere and over time simply withered from an evaporative process rather than rotting due to oxidation. Additional provisions included limited Martian grown vegetative food stuffs, based on genetic adaptations of Martian Maze, were quickly becoming an indispensable staple. Inside the dome all of the habitat modules, now in place were continually being fitted out and the last unit, dubbed the Martian Hilton was finally nearing completion. Guest rooms were bigger and lavishly decorated compared to the Spartan decor of the typical living quarters, and a rotating house-keeping and culinary staff provided an earth like hotel experience with an incomparable view. Open space under the dome was dominated by a town square in the center consisting of an amphitheater-lecture hall, visitor-hospitality center, a 360 degree IMAX movie theater, restaurant and alfresco dining, and a park area replete with wide swatches of Martian grass, benches and fountains providing a much needed humidification source for the entire facility. On the inside perimeter adjoining the habitat modules, a multi-use ½ mile jogging/biking path provided round the clock exercise opportunities for the entire community, although most of the field teams, working 12 hour days simply preferred to crash.

\Six months had passed since Arthur Daily's fatal visit to Alpha headquarters and Bob Tosky was finally on his way to Mars. Launched from our Cape Canaveral space port, the second flight of a newly redesigned ship was two days into its journey. The Jupiter series, although utilizing the same DREAM propulsion system as the Horizon craft, was radically different, employing two discrete sections; a cargo module considerably larger than its predecessor and an integrated, single transport module. Designed to achieve a higher level of autonomous flight controlled by an earth bound mission control and bigger and better passenger accommodations, Jupiter 2 began to mimic the luxury and comfort of a transatlantic zeppelin flight a century earlier. Arriving at one of several landing ports scattered around the outskirts of the city, Tosky was met by the new city administrator.

"Mr. Tosky glad to finally meet you, Jim Rheim at you service sir."

"No need to be so formal Jim, Bob suits me fine"… Jim smiled and nodded his head.

"Sure Bob, follow me I've got a transport waiting to take us into town." Driving thru an airlock into the dome, Tosky gawked like a kid first visiting Disney World,

"incredible Jim, just incredible, I've gone over these designs a thousand times and nothing, absolutely nothing prepares you for seeing it in person."

"Felt the same way when I first got here," Rheim replied, "but as they say, you ain't seen nothing yet….here's where you get off Bob, your room is ready and we have dinner reservations at Oglala Trattoria at seven."

A shower and short nap latter, Tosky felt unusually refreshed, even energetic following the week-long trip. Oglala Trattoria was located a short walk passed the hotel in the middle of an attractive court yard, and seemed to be a popular destination abuzz with lively chatter and music. Walking up to the reservation desk a well-dressed attendant cheerfully asked,

"Good evening, do you have a reservation?" Tosky grinned and looked awkward; he had to keep reminding himself that he was 80 million miles from home on an alien and supposedly uninhabited planet.

"Yes I believe the reservation name is under Rheim."

"Oh you must be Mr. Tosky; he's waiting for you - right this way sir." After dinner and an excellent bottle of wine, Jim Rheim carefully described on-going project details, schedules and technical issues, Tosky quietly listened until he was done.

"Jim I know you've got the talent to successfully manage these projects, that's what you're paid to do, ...but I'm not interested in your problems, I want to hear about my investments, what's our burn rate and when are we going to be profitable?" Taken by surprise at Tosky's candor, Rheim hesitated,

"I'll keep that in mind Bob, but I was informed that this was not a business trip and you were staying here as a visitor only." At those words Tosky's face began to glow red,

"Keep this in mind Rheim," Tosky began standing up, "I hired you and by God I can fire you..... Visitor or no visitor I'll expect to have financial results first thing in the morning." Not waiting for a reply he ended the conversation; "now if you'll excuse me I'm going back to my room....by the way, my compliments to the chef, dinner was superb." Sitting in the hotel lobby Tosky suddenly felt exhausted, the long trip and that out-burst on a full stomach drained him. Limping into his room he assured himself a good nights' rest was all he needed.

Mission control at the Cape was still in its formative stages despite the constant flight activities going on night and day. Now divided between commercial flights on one side of the base with public access and a separate, secure Government space port on the other side; NASA was quickly using up its existing fleet of rocket based vehicles while replacing them with DREAM powered ships. I was spending most of my time now at the Cape and planned on moving DREAM enterprises near there permanently. In addition to administrative duties shared with Tony Colby, most of the design decisions now found their way to my desk in Phil Visi's absence.

"Hello Bill, its Tom, you do know I have a partner in this enterprise… why are you forwarding all of the new design details to me?" Bill Heaney our flight director, had his own chain of command problems and was in no mood to handle someone else's,

"Because your partner doesn't have time to show up here anymore and flight can't authorize these changes without Visi's approval and in his absence you're the fall guy."

"That's terrific Bill, just what I need… is he still at his downtown office?"

"Oh I guess you haven't heard yet, his majesty opened up a high end think tank; hired some of the biggest names in physics, right here in the city."

"SON OF A BITCH; why the hell am I always the last one to know?"

"That's because you get the big bucks Tom," Heaney laughed, "I'll tell you this though, his new company has been re-computing all of our flight navigation data and its perfect, no more adjustments needed."

Phil Visi had been AWOL from the program for several months, struggling by himself to understand the celestial navigation problems we experienced in the Horizon flights. As a result of a hectic schedule I had lost touch while he was conducting most of his work at the Cape. Now in his new digs, and driven by a high profile research team, he was stirring up the scientific community, challenging widely held concepts of space-time and in particular gravitational effects on curved space. His new think tank was located in an up scaled business area, a 15 minute drive from Cape Canaveral. Phil was expecting me as I got off the elevator at the 10th floor.

"I meant to give you a heads up about all this Tom, but it just got away from me."

"I know the feeling buddy; I didn't realize you were gone until I got stuck with your work." Walking back to his office, Phil seemed excited.

"You wouldn't believe the reception I got after I published my navigation computations; I even got a letter from Stephen Hawking, said it made him reevaluate his black hole postulates. Can you believe that? He doesn't think they're relevant anymore." Startled by this and other responses from prestigious groups around the world, I began to understand the importance of the quest Phil had been laboring over for the past year.

"Congratulations Phil, it looks like you're really onto something, although I'm still not sure what it is - for my own sanity do you think you can leave out the math and explain it to me in layman's terms?"

"Sure Tom, just forget everything you thought you knew about Physics."

"I'm all ears partner; can't wait to hear this."

"As you know our flight plans had a few flaws in them and we needed to make several course corrections going to and from Mars…. So I began looking at the original calculations based on Special Relativity; its conventional wisdom for small objects like our ship, since gravitational effects can be excluded. Just for the hell of it I decided to redo the calculations based on General Relativity and some extremely small variations popped up that shouldn't have been there; even more surprising they only showed up when traveling at speeds approaching a million miles per hour. Using the course correction data from the Horizon flights, I was able to define the navigation calculations for the actual flight path. Surprisingly a perfect match was generated by slightly revising the Gravitational Constant that had been taken as Gospel for the past century."

"Jesus Phil, you're preaching heresy here, I'm surprised an international Physics mob hasn't tried to string you up yet."

"They were about to Tom, until guys like Hawking and a few other rebels came to my defense. We're floating a new unified field theory out there and its getting a lot of attention."

"Oh God this is worse than I thought; I know I'm in mortal danger now, so you may as well tell me the rest of the story."

"OK here's the short version. Immediately after the big bang the early expanse of space was filled with equal amounts of positive dark energy and negative dark energy. The universe was balanced and so-called gravitational forces were neutralized creating an uncomplicated steady state condition. Then nebulae from the big bang began to coalesce forming the planets, stars and galaxies and positive dark energy was the glue that held these bodies together. It's the reason why gasses and smaller objects clump together after colliding and once taken out of the equation, negative dark energy now acted as an unchecked universal force that we have been calling Gravity." When he finished I stared in disbelief at the audacity and genius of these ideas ......

"Son of a Bitch Phil, I knew it, I told you a long time ago there had to be a better explanation for Gravity and you found it".....

"No Tom, you found it in DREAM.....I only published it."

The week seemed endless and Friday came just in time; the upcoming short respite from a grinding work schedule raised my spirits. Getting ready to call it a day visitor control paged letting me know someone was waiting for me in the lobby. At the help desk I gestured questioningly to the attendant with open hands, as he pointed to a seating area occupied by a woman; she looked familiar and turning to face me I stopped in surprise.

"Hello stranger," she said, walking up to me - taking her hand I pulled her close and whispered,

"I didn't realize how much I missed you until now," and added, "but what the hell are you doing here Marie?"

"Why you... you inconsiderate man," she protested, pushing me away. "You left me alone for over a year, not even a phone call, nothing, and that's all you have to say; for all you care I could have been dead." Pulling her back I held her tightly in my arms;

"Don't say that Marie, it's not true; you know how I feel about you."

"I know, I know but you never tell me," she sobbed, "I missed you so much it hurts." The weekend we spent together was nothing short of a honeymoon. I had taken Marie for granted, thinking she would always be there for me. What I hadn't realized was how alone it made her feel.

"Marie you know I'm getting ready to move out here," I said getting dressed for work, "why don't you plan on relocating?"

"You see what I mean," she yelled, throwing a hair brush at me, "I'm not your pet, and I won't be treated like a plaything." Confused by her outburst I insisted,

"What the hell did I say?"

"It's not what you said….It's what you didn't say,"…. Pausing for a moment and thinking I had spent most of my adult life trying to understand women, never quite getting it right, but I did know one thing, it's not enough to love a woman they also want to be reminded that they are. Caressing her as she resisted looking away, I pulled her face to mine and said,

"I love you."

Arriving at mission control, the flight tower seemed eerily quiet, even somber.

"Good morning Bill," I cheerfully said and joked, "Who died?" Bill Heaney stared at me for a moment, long enough for me to know that something was really wrong.

"I'm sorry to be the bearer of bad news Tom…Bob Tosky took a massive heart attack last night."

"Oh my God is he alive?"

"Barely, the report we got said he was in critical condition; luckily one of the doctors that rotated to the Mars medical staff last month is a cardiologist. They also said that if he can be stabilized he really needs to be taken care of back here." Despite the news, our professionals, handling the nuts and bolts of the daily flight activity, shared a moment of silence and went right back to work knowing full well the lives of other people depended on their performance. The day passed without further incident, aside from hourly updates on Tosky's condition. The good news was he was breathing on his own now, but several specialized clot busting drugs needed to improve his condition were still 2 days away. Thinking there's nothing I could do about it, walking out to my car, my cell phone rang. It was a second shift flight engineer.

"Mr. D'Antonio I think you should get back here right away, we just had a serious in flight incident with Jupiter 7." Rushing back into the control tower, I could hear the communication chatter coming from Jupiter 7.

"What have we got?" I asked.

"A meteor strike, Mr. D'Antonio they couldn't have been more than 30 minutes into stage 2, when the collision occurred.

"How the hell could that happen? SOCAS or the plasma shield should have prevented it, were they operable?"

"All systems were a go, but there is a blind spot in our security blanket."

"What the hell are you talking about?" I skeptically asked. "Those systems covered 100 % of the ship."

"Yes but not at slower speeds, anything under 50,000 mph and we're vulnerable and this apparently was a one in a million shot." The conversation with the ship was constantly interrupted with damage reports and becoming desperate,

"Flight, we've lost #3 power panel,"

"Copy that J-7, can you switch to manual operation?"

"That's a negative flight, the meteor hit the connecting pinion and knocked it clean off, I repeat Power panel # 3 is gone,"…….

"Roger J-7, we'll get back to you shortly." Shaking his head the flight engineer looked worried, "they've got a really bad problem up there. If they can't correct their course soon we're gonna lose them." Bill Heaney arrived and after reviewing the communication log quickly issued instructions to the flight team trying to get control of the ship.

"Glad you're here Bill, do we have a solution?"

"Don't know yet Tom, but I do know that any software mods to fly the bird with a missing panel will have to come from here and even that's a long shot, no chance they can do it alone."

"What else Bill?" He hesitated…

"if we can't come up with a solution within 24 hours we'll lose the ship. Right now they're flying a spiral pattern; it's accelerating and going straight for the moon. In 24 hours they'll blow right by the moon traveling at over 100,000 mph and simply disappear in outer space somewhere. Then, if they're really lucky something else will hit them and destroy the ship."

"What about a high speed rescue mission?" I asked. "If we can intercept and push the bird around we'd have a chance."

"What chance Tom, we're 2 days away from getting the next ship ready for a launch, not to mention a crew, and how the hell do we grab hold of the bird? At those speeds any collision would be a disaster."

Sitting in my office I was watching the night sky imagining the anguish the crew of Jupiter 7 was going thru. Theirs would not be a quick death only an interminable out of control journey to nowhere. Stretching my arms to relax my shoulders I accidentally knocked over model vehicles on my desk. There on one edge of the desk was a Jupiter model, held up from falling by a sky crane model wedged under its side. The idea hit me like a smack in the face – the sky crane was practically designed for this – it had the grappling and lift capability, as well as the speed, and more importantly could be readied for flight within an hour.

"Bill," I yelled excitedly over the phone, "the sky crane, we need a sky crane for a rescue." The phone was silent for a long moment.

"Damn Tom, why didn't I think of that, Damn good idea,… we have a few vehicles on the training line right now, only trouble is they're in South Dakota."

"Call them Bill, right now, ask for volunteers and don't minimize the situation." Within minutes after the request went out, my cell phone rang,

"Tom its Joe, I heard about the problem,"

"Yea this is a tough one Joe where are you?"

"I'm in South Dakota, and in case you didn't know it I'm now a certified sky crane jockey." I knew from the tone in his voice what he was implying.

"No Joe this is a job for the younger guys, you won't be able to tolerate it."

"Tom listen to me, I want this, it's my chance, don't take it away from me."

The sky crane team in South Dakota was immediately mobilized, as a stand by vehicle was being programmed with the latest telemetry from Jupiter 7. Joe Campo got his wish; he was selected as the primary pilot and given the nature of the mission, without objection. The sky crane would have to launch within the hour for an 8 hour intercept flight, reaching Jupiter 7 less than 40,000 miles above the surface of the moon. At intercept it was expected that J-7 would be traveling at over 75,000 mph while the sky crane dubbed Rescue 1 would reach a maximum velocity of 300,000 mph before slamming on the brakes. After maneuvering into a synchronous flight path with J-7 contact would have to occur, literally within minutes, stopping and redirecting the ship to avoid crashing on the moon. Shortly after launch flight management would be transferred to mission control at the Cape allowing a few minutes of downtime and casual chatter before fully reengaging in the upcoming chase.

"Joe we'll get you to the target so don't worry about navigation, focus on planning your intercept maneuvers based on telemetry updates; you'll only get one shot at this."

"Copy that Tom. By the way I've sent you a very important letter for safekeeping until I return."

"What letter, what are you talking about?" "Tom please listen we don't have much time, it's only to be opened if I don't return."

"Nonsense buddy you'll be back and I'll owe you a dinner."

"I'm planning on it Tom, but promise me you'll do this," again I paused for a moment, Leary of its contents...

"Sure Joe, I'll hold your letter."

The bright Martian sunlight filtered into the intensive care unit, as Bob Tosky blinked and squinted at the nurse at his side.

"How long have I been here?" he asked, in a barely audible tone."

"Two days now Mr. Tosky, please try to remain still, we've got an assist pump on your femoral artery. It's helping your heart rest so it can heal." Tosky looked away, more annoyed at his condition than concerned.

"Can't be that bad, I feel OK. Besides I'm getting hungry."

"That's good to hear Mr. Tosky, if you're up to it you can have visitors; is there anybody you'd like to see?" Motioning the nurse to come closer

"Call Jim Rheim," he growled as loud as he could, "tell him to get his ass over here." The whole city was now aware of the drama that was unfolding near the moon and it was particularly distracting to the new administrator having a close personal friend on board Jupiter 7. Nevertheless Bob Tosky was a VIP and despite any personal reservations, he would be treated as such while visiting his city.

"Good afternoon Bob," Jim said in an up-beat tone of voice. "For as sick as your chart says, you certainly look good." Tosky grinned,

"Yea we'll you better do something about that restaurant, another meal like that and I'm a goner." Both men laughed for a moment as the look on Tosky's face became serious.

"What's this emergency that everybody's whispering about - something about a lunar landing?"

"You don't need to concern yourself about that now Bob."

"Jim you have a habit of saying the wrong things to me."

"I only meant," Jim started to protest…Tosky held his hand up,

"I know what you meant, save the bullshit, just tell me what's really going on."

Rescue 1 was quickly closing on Jupiter 7 while Joe Campo was getting ready to manually execute a tricky synchronizing maneuver. Now paralleling J-7's spiraling flight path, less than 25 meters away, the sky crane slowly closed on the ship for the first attempt at docking.

"We're tracking now Rescue 1,…15 meters and closing."

"Copy that Flight; I'm shooting for the first hard point on the port side of Cargo, once I lock on you'll have to guide me the rest of the way; I won't have a visual on the second."

"Roger that Rescue 1, will advise." A few moments later Joe's voice crackled over the intercom,

"CONTACT, hold, hold, and…hard dock, I've got hard dock flight." A low cheer echoed thru mission control,

"That's affirmative Rescue 1, great job Joe." As flight continued to direct Joe's maneuvers, I was focused on velocity;

"Bill, look at their speed," I said in an anxious tone of voice, "we need to start decelerating now."

"We'll be ready in two minutes," he intently replied."

"BILL" I hollered, "look at their trajectory, they don't have two minutes." Looking up at the big board he winced,

"Christ almighty, RESCUE 1, RESCUE 1, go for docking immediately, I repeat immediately." Half way thru the final maneuver the second docking point was barely visible; abandoning his carefully choreographed approach Joe jerked the grappling arm in the direction of the hard point;

"no good, no good," he yelled, "I'm resetting the arm for another try." Breaking protocol I began using an open communication link.

"Joe you're out of time; abort the rescue; get the hell out of there."

"Almost there Tom, just a few more feet,…almost there….GOT IT, hard dock!"

"JOE START DECELERATION NOW," I yelled watching the lunar surface coming up fast; "FULL POWER JOE, FULL POWER." Thirty seconds later, Jupiter 7 reported in,

"Touchdown Flight. We had a hard landing but the ship is intact."

"That's affirmative Jupiter 7 you've got a bunch of guys down here breathing again.

"Rescue 1, Come in…..Come in Rescue 1,,….Rescue 1 Come in……..Come in Rescue 1……Do you copy, come in, come in Rescue 1….. Only a low frequency hum and intermittent static was the reply. The silence filled me with dread, realizing what just happened; the sky crane took the brunt of the crash and the communication link was dead, and so was my boyhood friend.

A week later the Jupiter 7 crew, along with Joe's body was retrieved. I gave the eulogy, a hero's ceremony attended by the entire Cape facility; its main space port now renamed Campo Station. Joe made the ultimate sacrifice. He gave his life so that others may live and in the process earned the redemption he so desperately wanted. Mourning the death of my friend I almost forgot the letter he mysteriously asked me to hold. Quietly alone in my office I held the letter in my hand wondering about its content, as I slit open the flap of the envelope a single page neatly folded fell out:

> Tom if you're reading this letter the worst has happened and I am not returning from the mission. Some time ago Jim Dougherty and I were involved in a shooting that killed an Aerospace executive by name of Jack Bickford. Although, in my opinion the killing was justified I wanted you to know that it was I who fired the fatal shots. Making this confession, I am of sound mind and body. In my death Tom, I did not want to burden my soul without admitting my guilt. Please provide this confession to the proper authorities so that this case may be closed and provide some relief to the remaining family members.

> Goodbye Tom, thanks for your understanding -- Joe

Putting the letter down I began to smile at the irony; Joe had not only saved the lives of his fellow crewmen he also found a way to release Jim Dougherty and Sue Lee from a self-imposed prison. However comfortable Mars could become, it was still no earth and certainly not yet a place to raise a child.

The upheaval of the past year coupled with my incessant travel schedule was driving ArmorTec's relocation ahead of schedule. Our New Jersey facility had been sold to a private developer months before and was scheduled for demolition as soon as the property was vacated. We had originally planned to allow a 3 month transition but now, fast tracking the transfer of personnel and equipment I was about to close the doors one final time. Arriving at Philly International a cab dropped me off at ArmorTec late in the afternoon. Janitorial personnel were just finishing up as I entered the building.

"Why hello Mr. D'Antonio, I didn't expect to see you around here anymore."

"Just wanted to do a final inspection Nelson," I said to the man who meticulously cleaned and maintained the property for the past 25 years, "what do you think you'll do after we close?" Nelson smiled and rubbed his head,

"Don't really know, I've never been out of work before. I've got a sister in South Carolina, thought I'd move in with her, at least for a while anyway. I'm sure gonna miss the action around here though."

"That's right Nelson, I almost forgot, you probably know more about what went on in here than I do." Agreeing, Nelson shook his head,

"I'll bet you don't remember your first Government contract audit."

"Actually I do Nelson; as I recall we made a hell of a lot of money and expected to get slammed for excess profits. We got lucky, the auditor never said a word." Slapping his leg and laughing out loud, Nelson continued,

"What you didn't know was that your auditor was a closet alcoholic. The first night there he got stoned and accidentally dumped all of his work in the trash. When I arrived the next night he pleaded with me to try and recover the report. It was gone and I figured he was too embarrassed to raise the issue at all."

"Son of a bitch, I never did understand why that happened," and do you remember.............the two men continued exchanging stories for an hour reliving ArmorTec's history, both the good and bad and how it affected their lives.

Evening shadows began invading the building as the day slipped away. Alone now I walked into my office, touching the walls. Standing there in the silence I could almost hear the memories and imagined my old friends thru the dust particles in the air reflecting the fading sunlight. The reverie tired my soul and I felt a curious sadness. Turning around I thought I saw the illusion of a woman in the doorway and reaching out to the shadow Marie's face came into view in the dim sunlight,

"Marie, is that you?"

"Hi handsome, yes it's me; I was afraid you had forgotten your way around. Thought I'd stop by and give you the cook's tour."

"Yea… somehow you always did know when I need you."

"It's an old habit Tom, second nature to me now." Walking out the door, arm-in-arm for the last time I looked up into a moon lit sky;

"it's getting late Marie, don't you think we should be going home?" She stopped and stared at me as her eyes began to moisten,

"You never said that to me before," and added in a quivering voice, "I don't know where that is." Holding her close and wiping a tear from her face, I whispered,

"Honey, from now on I don't care where we are…. as long as I'm with you I am home."

- The End -

Epilogue

40 years have passed since the first Martian landing and most of the pioneers that made it happen are gone now. The build-up and expansion of Martian communities continued unabated thru the years and over 100 new cities now occupied the planet's landscape put there by both private and Government agencies from around the world. In some ways these new communities far exceeded the allure and attraction of earth born metropolises. People were bound to each other now like never before and race and culture didn't matter. All were explorers on a common mission, to carve out a new home as the indigenous inhabitants of an alien planet, the first citizens of Mars.

Bob Tosky survived his heart attack and refusing to be ambulanced back to earth, recovered during his stay on Mars. In typical fashion he quickly became a driving force in the development of Oglala City and other communities and eventually became the first Governor of a collection of colonies, named the "United Cities of Mars." Presiding over a transportation revolution both on Earth and Mars, he truly lived his dreams right up to the end, having had his body launched out of our solar system and beyond powered by the inexhaustible energy of DREAM.

Sue Lee and Jim Dougherty safely returned to earth and married and remaining an intimate part of our earth based Martian community, both continued to work at Mission Control in Cape Canaveral. Sue, still attached to the medical staff at the Cape, continues to contribute her unique expertise. Jim has since passed, but survived by his son Sean, his legacy was not forgotten now filling the role of flight director at Mission Control.

Phil Visi continued on in his quest to rewrite the laws of Physics. After forming a collaborative relationship with Stephen Hawking his star quality took off, revising the structure of Black Holes. He eventually got his Nobel Prize but more importantly he followed his dreams and led the life he was so ably born for.

Tony Colby retired a second time to private life. Called upon by some of his Government contacts looking to take advantage of the Martian hype, he entered the lecture circuit in and around the DC area. Soon the demand for his lectures and stories exceeded all expectation and unwittingly became a space based cult legend, having never traveled to Mars.

Joe Campo remained in our minds and hearts long after he was gone. The crash site on the moon was dedicated as a monument to the courage of a man, seeking redemption and willing to pay the ultimate price. Joe was not at all the hero type, but it is a testament to the spirit of the common man that when called upon in the direst of circumstances he truly becomes exceptional.

Tom D'Antonio and Marie married and continued living near the cape after retiring from the grueling schedule of running a space based industry. It's a young man's job, he would say, disguising his temporary regrets each time he visited mission control. Throughout the rest of his life a seat for him was always left next to the flight director at mission control and although empty now it still remains in honor of a man that caught the brass ring on a merry go round and never let go.

Printed in the United States
By Bookmasters